All the air whoos[h] as he looked at

Samantha Harcourt. The [...]
He'd nearly made a foo[l...]
actually prayed for God to send her back after that
amazing day.

Now back in the States, he found her picture was
everywhere. Billboards, magazines.

He'd had no idea the sweet missions worker was a
top model. Once he'd discovered her identity, he'd felt
like an idiot. He'd also understood why she'd never
returned. She wasn't a missions worker at all. Like all
celebrities, she loved publicity. What better press than
to say she'd worked among the orphans of Africa?

Wasn't this newspaper photo proof enough?

Sam Harcourt was back in town.

* * *

**A Tiny Blessings Tale: Loving families and
needy children continue to come together
to fulfill God's greatest plans!**

Books by Linda Goodnight

Love Inspired

In the Spirit of…Christmas #326
A Very Special Delivery #349
*A Season for Grace #377
*A Touch of Grace #390
*The Heart of Grace #401
Missionary Daddy #408

*The Brothers' Bond

LINDA GOODNIGHT

A romantic at heart, Linda Goodnight believes in the traditional values of family and home. Writing books enables her to share her certainty that, with faith and perseverance, love can last forever and happy endings really are possible.

A native of Oklahoma, Linda lives in the country with her husband, Gene, and Mugsy, an adorably obnoxious rat terrier. She and Gene have a blended family of six grown children. Linda is an elementary school teacher, as well as a licensed nurse. When time permits, Linda loves to read, watch football and rodeo, and indulge in chocolate. She also enjoys taking long, calorie-burning walks in the nearby woods. Readers can write to her at linda@lindagoodnight.com, or c/o Steeple Hill Books, 233 Broadway, Suite 1001, New York, NY 10279.

Missionary Daddy
Linda Goodnight

Steeple
Hill®

Published by Steeple Hill Books™

Special thanks and acknowledgment are given to
Linda Goodnight for her contribution to the
A TINY BLESSINGS TALE miniseries.

STEEPLE HILL BOOKS

Steeple
Hill®

ISBN-13: 978-0-373-87444-6
ISBN-10:   0-373-87444-8

MISSIONARY DADDY

Man looks at the outward appearance,
but the Lord looks at the heart.
—*I Samuel* 16:7

Acknowledgments

A special thanks to my daughter, Sundy,
for sharing her experiences as a missionary
to Africa as well as her counseling expertise
with those suffering from anorexia and bulimia.
Also to fellow writer and former model
Terri Reed, and to another writing buddy,
Shirley Jump, whose years in the television
industry provided the finishing touches.

And as always, to the children of the world
who wait. I'm praying for you.

Chapter One

One year ago, Africa

"I'm going. Either with you or alone, but I'm going."

A determined Samantha Harcourt ignored her driver's coming protest and slipped into the back seat of the tiny European car. After three days on the South African coast, she'd seen nothing but the posh resort hotels along the ruggedly beautiful beaches. The real Africa was out there somewhere and she aimed to see it. Today.

Alfred, the ebony-faced driver, had driven her and the other models around the private beach areas rented by *Sports Stuff Magazine* for their annual swimsuit edition, but no one else had requested to go beyond the tourist areas. Even now, with the modeling shoot about to wrap and go back to America, the other models lounged on the white sand beaches, uninterested in the rest of the country.

"I may only be here once, Alfred. Please. I want to see the real Africa."

The man sat like a stone at the wheel.

"I was instructed not to take you there," he said, his accent an interesting mix of African dialect and clipped British tones.

Sam sighed and peeled off a hundred-rand note, offering it without further comment.

Alfred shook his head but took the money and cranked the engine.

Satisfied, Samantha sat back to enjoy the scenery, digital camera at ready. She wasn't sure what to expect. Her life as a fashion model had taken her around the world and to many diverse places, but this was her first trip to Africa.

"Do you know a market where I can buy a ceremonial mask?" She collected masks of all kinds and would love one from this continent.

Alfred's dark eyes flashed in the mirror. "I will get you a mask. The markets aren't safe for tourists."

Sam figured that was the best she could hope for. "I'd appreciate that, Alfred. Thank you."

"We go back now. Yeah."

She'd been warned that the crime rate was high in some areas, but...

"I want to see where the everyday people of Africa live."

Alfred's wrinkled brow deepened to cornrows, but he drove on.

Within ten minutes, she understood his reluctance. Wealthy mansions gave way to shanties—

makeshift dwellings patched together with cardboard, tin, bricks and a hodgepodge of found materials.

Poverty, astonishing and terrible, spread out in a wide swath. Bony children played in the unending dirt with sticks and rocks. Adolescent girls carried water from muddy ponds while women hung meager laundry across strips of bowing rope or string. It was a scene of inexpressible squalor.

A deep sense of shame shifted over Sam, so profound that her stomach rolled. All she'd ever done was pose for a camera and look pretty. In her entire life, she'd done nothing that mattered. Yet she had so much, and these people had so little.

"We go back now? Yeah," Alfred said again.

Sam turned horrified eyes to him. "No. Keep driving."

Something inside her was stirring, some innate longing. Turning back now was out of the question.

In the distance, a ways from the bulk of the desolate township, she spotted activity of a different kind. Someone was constructing a building.

Leaning forward, Sam squinted toward the structure. Habitat for Humanity, perhaps? Did they work in foreign lands?

She pointed. "Take me there."

"The American missionary." Alfred nodded, this time approving her idea. "He is building a fine, new orphanage for the little ones."

An orphanage. Children without families. Sam gripped the edge of the window; the inner churning grew worse by the minute. Her family hadn't been that supportive, but she'd grown up with every material advantage. She could barely conceive of children with nothing to depend upon but the kindness of strangers.

She glanced down at her acrylic nails, safari shorts and designer top. A pair of gold bracelets—twenty-four carat speckled with costly gems—jangled at her wrist. Matching earrings dangled from her ears. Her tiny bag was Gucci, her sandals Prada. Her clothes and jewelry would probably pay for building that small orphanage. This morning the attire had been perfection, a reflection of the persona she cultivated. Now, the shallow trappings of a pampered life brought only shame.

Eric Pellegrino thought the African sun had finally gotten to him. Standing with a brick in one hand and a trowel in the other, he stared at the tall blond apparition stepping out of the tiny car. Dust swirled up around her, making the scene even more surreal. A mirage. That was what she had to be. Not the team leader who'd been felled by traveling sickness.

"Eric, Eric." Amani, the six-year-old orphan boy who had long since won his heart, came running around the side of the building. His little brother, Matunde, only three, ran behind him. Amani pointed to the car. "Company. More workers."

Both boys clapped their hands with glee and rushed the vehicle.

Eric figured he should close his gaping mouth and go rescue the woman before Matunde and Amani scared her off. Missions' teams arrived every summer to help the orphanage on a short-term basis, mostly youth groups with little knowledge but great enthusiasm. This year they were adding on to the tiny, overcrowded orphanage.

One thing he'd learned after nearly six years in Africa, never turn down a gift or an offer of help. If she was here, she must be feeling better.

He was the one suffering from a sudden attack of breathlessness.

He handed the mudded brick to one of the teens and went to greet the newcomer. The orphans, always fascinated by a vehicle or company, swarmed the car. When several children wrapped around her legs, the woman bent low and hugged them. Eric's heart bumped. Anyone who cared about the kids was automatically on his happy list.

His newest helper was tall and tan and willowy, pale blond hair slicked back from a clean, natural face into a thick ponytail. Elegantly groomed eyebrows arched above a pair of stunning silver-blue eyes that gazed at him with undisguised interest. With her delicate beauty and her fancy clothes, she looked as out of place as a princess at a mud-wrestling contest.

He, who'd learned the hard way not to be misled by exterior appearances, couldn't stop staring.

Sure, she was beautiful, but the instant connection was more than that. It was as if he knew her already, as if he knew the things that would make her laugh…and cry, as if he looked into the face of his future.

With a shake of his head, he dispelled the odd sensation and stepped forward.

"I'm Eric," he said. "Director here. These are my kids. Or rather the orphanage charges. I call them my kids."

Smiling down at the children, the mirage untangled herself and offered a well-groomed hand. "I'm Sam."

Her skin felt the way he'd known it would. Soft and pampered, but under-girded with steel, even if those fingernails wouldn't last ten minutes. "Welcome to Ithemba House. Feeling better?"

She blinked at him. "I beg your pardon?"

Matunde and Amani already had her hands, tugging toward the structure.

"The mission's director called. Said you were under the weather. International travel does that to a lot of people."

"Oh. Right. Sure. I—" She looked around at the driver and then back at Eric. A strange expression, almost of decision, came and went. Eric understood. She wouldn't be the first who was scared off by the sheer enormity of the problems he faced every day. But Eric hoped she would stay for more reasons than he could articulate.

Finally, she let the boys pull her forward. "So where do I start?"

Eric jerked his head toward the building. Even seriously overdressed for the task, the woman had grit. He liked her attitude. Ah, who was he kidding?

Sam intrigued and attracted him. There was something very special about her. "Some of the other girls are around back mixing mud for the bricks."

As much as he'd like to forget work today and spend it getting to know her better, they had a job to do. He figured a job away from him was the best place for lovely Sam.

"Okay," she said. "Just a second." With the boys in tow, she went back to the car and spoke to the driver. From the man's expression, he wasn't happy with his passenger, but he nodded and drove away.

Led by the adorable little boys, Sam joined the group of laughing, sweating teens at the far end of the orphanage. Though she'd never done construction work, neither had any of the other girls. And she was a master at faking it. With no regard to her clothes or her jewelry, she set to work. The workers were chatty, and quickly filled her in on their African adventure. Having only just arrived, they were from a church in Texas that supported the orphanage on a regular basis.

When she brought the topic around to the missionary, a couple of the girls giggled. One said, "Cute, huh?"

Sam only smiled but she had to agree. Eric was not only darkly handsome, he radiated a contagious charm and energy. She thought it was funny that he had mistaken her for one of these kids, considering she was nearly twenty-seven and they were all teenagers. But she let the misunderstanding ride, embarrassed to admit what she did for a living. He'd probably sneer if she told him. Compared to his work, hers was meaningless.

Stirring a bucket of a substance resembling white concrete, she glanced Eric's way. At any one time, several small children swarmed around him, pulling on his legs and arms. Over and over, with infinite patience, he stopped whatever he was doing to acknowledge them. And she'd never seen anyone work so hard and laugh so much.

Eric was a very interesting man. And she wanted to know him better, if for no other reason than to understand more about the mission.

As he struggled to lift an oversized window into place, Sam saw her chance and hurried over to help him hoist one side.

"Looks like you could use an extra hand."

"Thanks," he grunted as together they shoved the framed glass into the open wall. "This window is bigger than usual but electricity here is iffy. We need the sunlight for the kids' studies."

"The kids go to school here?"

"Yep. No place else to go."

Sam leaned her body weight against the window frame while Eric made adjustments. "How many kids live here?"

"Ten." He used his fist to pound a corner into the tight space. "But as soon as these new rooms are ready we can take in twenty more plus two caregivers."

She was horrified. "Are there that many orphans?"

"Not even a drop in the bucket to the number out there with no place to go." He motioned with his chin. "Hand me that bag of nails, will you?"

Sam complied and found herself assisting him as he hammered the window into the wall. Her mind couldn't wrap itself around the idea of so many children alone.

"How do you do this? I mean, there's so much need."

"It's tough sometimes, but I love what I do." He wiped a muscled forearm across a face damp with hard work and summer heat. "Africa has taught me to trust God. Really trust Him. When we need something, He always comes through."

Well, what had she expected? The man *was* a missionary. Sam, who wasn't sure what she believed, had never been a religious person, had never been around any to speak of, though her sister Ashley had become a Christian after the birth of her son a couple of years ago. Sam was still curious about that turn of events.

"How long have you been here?"

"Nearly six years."

"All that time." She was amazed. Years without microwaves or hot showers or air-conditioning.

She took the extra hammer and tried to drive a nail. It bent double. "Do you ever go home?"

"I furlough at least once a year. Lately—" His face clouded for a second as if he wanted to share something worrisome. But instead he shook his head and laughed. "I see you've done a lot of carpentry work."

Sam grinned. "Tons. Can't you tell by my finesse?"

Eyes twinkling, the charming missionary flipped

his hammer around to the claw end and extracted the nail with one fluid twitch of a powerful wrist.

"I know you're a master craftsman and all," he said, still grinning, "but let me show you the way we poor African missionaries hammer a nail."

"I'm all ears," she answered, extending the hammer. "Or maybe I should say all thumbs?"

Eric made a huffing noise in appreciation of her humor. Sam's mood spiraled upward. She liked this guy.

"Strike with your arm, not your wrist. You'll get more power that way," he was saying as he leaned in from behind to demonstrate the correct way to hold a hammer.

"Where are you from, Sam?" Eric asked as they worked.

"Chicago. Virginia, originally. Why?"

He tilted his head. "You don't exactly look like the missions type. What do you do back in Chicago?"

A frisson of embarrassment kept her from telling him. Her work was so superficial. "Just a job. Nothing special."

But what Eric did *was* special. The most special work she'd ever witnessed. This man and his team of helpers were making a difference in human lives every single day.

Together they finished securing the window. A couple of teenage boys came around the building to inquire about lunch.

"The food bus arrives at noon," Eric told them. "They should be here any minute."

"Don't you have food here?"

"Sure, but we'll eat later. The food van is for the others."

Sam didn't recall seeing any others, but she didn't argue on a day filled with interesting occurrences.

The sun was high in the sky and the heat scorching, much hotter than along the beach. Even though she was an exercise fiend, Sam doubted if she'd ever perspired quite this much. She pulled her damp cotton shirt away from her body, letting cool air rush in. She should be exhausted and ready to escape. Instead she felt an energy rush and deep satisfaction.

A white van chugged down the road, horn blaring in a jolly rhythm. Suddenly, the landscape erupted with humanity, mostly children. They came running from all directions, feet bare, clothes in pitiful condition, smiles wide, carrying containers of every sort from a regular bowl to a discarded lid.

The teenagers appeared as startled as Sam. Eric clapped his hands and motioned toward the awning being erected by staff members. The chattering children crowded in to sit on the hard-packed ground.

During the next few minutes, Eric, with children in his lap and hanging over his back, spoke to the group about Jesus's love for them. The simple, sweet, spiritual message brought a lump to Sam's throat. She hoped it was true. These precious babies needed someone big and strong to love them.

Two of the teenagers from the mission team presented a children's song, urging the sea of faces to sing and clap. Laughter and energy rippled through the clearing. For all the despair, these people could still find joy, something sorely missing in her life most of the time.

A child no more than three had chosen Sam's lap and cuddled close to play with her shining bracelets. Flies swarmed, the sun scorched and dirt was everywhere. But Sam was oddly content.

When the brief Bible lesson ended, a makeshift table was loaded with an enormous pot of porridge-looking stuff.

"Can you handle this?" Eric asked, offering the ladle to Sam.

"I may not be able to hammer but I can dip," she said and was rewarded with his wide grin.

"I knew you were a talented woman. Today the dipper. Tomorrow the roof."

Tomorrow. She didn't know how to tell him there would be no tomorrow.

A sea of thin, hungry faces swarmed the table, bowls upraised, amazingly considerate of one another. Though clearly in need of food, no one pushed the other out of the way. Most even took their meager rations and headed home to share with other family members. When Sam heard that, she almost cried.

The rest of the group handed out slices of white bread while she filled containers. Eric worked beside the orphan children, quietly directing them to be of service to the others. Not a one argued or insisted on eating first.

Sam dipped until the pot emptied. Still the children came.

"We need more," she said.

The van driver shrugged. "There is no more."

With a sinking feeling, she scraped the remains into one final cup and watched with heavy heart as the latecomers trudged away empty-handed but uncomplaining. The message was clear: such was the way of life in Africa.

Eric appeared at her side and draped an arm comfortingly over her shoulders. He brought with him the pleasant scent of healthy, hardworking male. "You can't let it get to you."

Hot and sticky and sad, she stared bleakly at the last child ambling down the dusty road, empty container dangling from his fingertips. "Some went away hungry."

"But many didn't. You have to look at the good you've done instead of what you can't do. That's Africa."

"Can't we get more food out here?" She had money. She could buy whatever they needed.

"The town missionaries bring what they can every day, but they have people inside the city to feed, as well."

She had to find a way to help. To make a difference in these precious lives. Maybe she couldn't change things today, but some day…

"Come on," Eric said. "Zola has lunch for the rest of us inside."

Food held no appeal for Samantha. These children needed to eat far more than she did. She pinched the skin on her upper arm, dismayed to find a fleshy strip of triceps. The negative voices started up inside her head. *Too fat. Ugly. Worthless.*

With the skills she'd developed over several years of coping, she pushed the thoughts away and concentrated on feeding the orphans. According to the doctors, her weight was finally at a semi-healthy level, whether she believed it or not.

Along toward sunset, a van rattled down the road to take the teenagers back to their base camp inside the city.

Sam didn't go with them.

"The driver who brought me is coming back later," she said.

That was fine with Eric. He could use her help getting the kids washed, read to and down for the night. And he enjoyed the prospect of spending a little one-on-one time with the sweet and lovely Samantha. Broken fingernails aside, she'd proven herself to be a real trooper all day.

"I've never seen anything quite so brave and wonderful as these children," Sam said later as they settled outside in the evening with bottles of clean water. Even the water struck her as more significant than ever before. Here, water was at a premium all the time.

Eric angled toward her in the semidarkness, water bottle dangling from one hand. "They were fascinated with your hair. I doubt they'd ever seen so much long, straight, white hair. It was nice of you to let them touch it."

Her ponytail had long since pulled loose on the sides and Eric was as tempted as the children to get his hands on the flowing blond silk.

She brushed the strands back with both hands. "I didn't mind. The kids are adorable."

"So what do you think of Africa so far?"

The easy smile disappeared. "The people are gentle and friendly, but the poverty is unbelievable. And the orphans…"

Eric knew exactly what she meant. Sometimes the conditions overwhelmed. If God hadn't called him here, he would have given up a long time ago. But the Lord and his heart wouldn't let him.

"Every day the problem grows worse. More parents die of AIDS or malaria. More children left alone. The African people take care of one another when they can, but most barely survive. How can they take in an orphaned child?"

He shook his head, aware that the worry he hid from the kids had seeped through.

Sam's smooth, soft hand touched his. "Your work here is wonderful, Eric. You're doing all you possibly can."

But it wasn't enough.

Sweet Sam was trying to encourage him and the thought both moved and amused Eric. He was generally the comforter, the strong one. But he was grateful that God had sent this particular missions' worker halfway across the world just when he needed encouragement.

"If only those with the financial means would do

more," he muttered. But in his experience, the rich just got richer. Africa was proof of that. "You drove through the townships to get here. You saw the line between the haves and have-nots—a mansion on one side of the road and hovels on the other."

"It's shocking, isn't it?"

Resentment burned the back of his throat like acid. "There are people in this country wealthy enough to solve the hunger problem, yet they won't even cross the road to offer a loaf of bread to a needy family."

It was the regular working folks, grandmas on fixed incomes, people of modest means who supported the fatherless. They were the ones with compassion. The wealthy of the world were too busy blessing themselves.

"The Bible said it's easier for a camel to go through the eye of a needle than for a rich man to enter heaven. All you have to do is look around to understand that."

Sam had grown very quiet and Eric regretted his outburst. He bumped her hand with his water bottle. "Sorry. I didn't need to dump my worries on you."

"It's okay." But her soft voice held a sadness he couldn't interpret.

For the past few months he'd been contemplating a decision about his work here. He'd prayed and studied the Bible, asked for opinions from the missions' board and the African consulate. Still, he hadn't decided how best to help the orphans he loved so much. Sometimes the frustration with people who *could* give and didn't built up until he said too much.

"The orphanage meets the basic needs," he said. "We teach them about Jesus, love them all we can, but children need more. They need families."

"Matunde and Amani seem to think you *are* their family."

He chuckled softly. "I guess I am. They've been with me since their mother died when Matunde was born. Afterward, I won their father to the Lord. When he got sick, too, he brought baby Matunde and his big brother here."

"And you took them in."

He took a swig from his water bottle, remembering the desperately ill man, weak and gaunt, who'd walked miles to ensure his children would be cared for. "It was their father's last request. I couldn't refuse, even though we normally refer infants to a baby hospital. In fact, Matunde was the first and only baby we've had here."

"That's why he's crazy about you. You probably diapered the little guy."

"I did. Clumsy as an ox, but he and I muddled through until Zola came along to help."

Perhaps that was the reason he was so attached to the two brothers. He was the only parent they remembered. The thought of leaving behind tore at him like tiger's claws. The boys were part of his indecision.

"What you do is amazing. A true gift. I wish—" She let the thought trail away, saying instead, "How much longer until the construction is complete?"

"A week maybe. Mission teams generally work fast. All of you are doing a great job."

She held up her bruised thumb. "You call this great?"

"Sure," he said, bumping her with his shoulder. "A regular, *bang-up* job."

She rolled her silvery eyes, but they both chuckled softly at the joke.

"Why do you call the orphanage Ithemba House?"

"*Ithemba* means hope in several African languages. Sometimes hope is all I can give them."

"Hope is everything, Eric," she said in a soft voice. "Absolutely everything."

And he knew that Sam understood what so many others didn't about missionary work. Without the hope that God had a plan and purpose even for the lowliest, humankind was lost.

Night sounds closed in around them. The symphony of a dozen frog species. The clear, pure trill of night birds. The calls and cries of nocturnal creatures on the move. Noises as familiar to Eric as the lilting cadence of the many African dialects.

A scream ripped the darkness. Sam yipped and clutched his arm. "What was that?"

The eerie howl and piercing scream came again.

Sam had moved so close, Eric was reluctant to answer. But in fairness, he admitted, "A jackal. No harm to us."

He felt her relax, but she didn't scoot away and he was glad. They sat close, her hand on his arm.

"The stars look so near," she whispered. "I feel as if I can reach out and touch them."

"Want me to get one for you?"

She turned her head the slightest bit, bringing her face close. Her full, bowed lips lifted in a soft smile.

"Would you?"

He was a missionary, a man not given to impulse, a man very careful not to overstep his bounds, but he wanted to kiss the lovely Sam.

He shifted around toward her, lifting one hand to brush a stray lock behind her ear. As he'd expected, her hair was silk. In the moonlight, their eyes met and held.

Then the sweep of car lights found them and Eric moved away, both thankful and sorry for the interruption.

"There's my ride," Sam said. Eric leaped to his feet and helped her up. Her skin, even after a hard day's work, was as silky as her hair. Regretfully, that would change by the time her mission team left Africa.

They walked to the car, still holding hands.

"Thanks for your help today."

She shook her head. "No. Thank you. I learned so much. I never—" Her voice choked. Eric moved closer, but Sam backed away and reached for the car door. "Bye, Eric. Today was wonderful."

As the car pulled out, Eric raised a hand. "See you tomorrow."

But he didn't. In fact, Samantha never returned to the orphanage again. Eric was not only disappointed, he was bewildered to learn that Sam was not a part of the missions' team. The team didn't know her any more than he did.

No one could figure exactly what had happened. One thing for certain, she'd made an impression on him.

Eric spent a couple of days talking to God about the incident. Because for that one, beautiful day, he had almost believed in love at first sight.

And he didn't even know her last name.

Chapter Two

Present day, Chestnut Grove, Virginia

His dream was coming true.

Eric Pellegrino sat at the desk inside the offices of Tiny Blessings Adoption Agency reading the home study of a prospective adoptive family.

Last year, after much prayer and counsel, he'd resigned his work in Africa to take the job as assistant director in charge of developing an international adoption program for Tiny Blessings. Now that the director, Kelly Van Zandt was pregnant and had cut back on her hours, he was heavily involved in all aspects of the agency, but his dream of finding permanent families for the orphans of Africa never left his thoughts.

Matunde and Amani were waiting. And the paperwork to make them his official children now awaited approval from the South African government. If all went well, other orphans would also soon be crossing the waters to loving families.

He completed his notes on the prospective parents and slid their information into a file. They, too, were interested in adopting from Africa.

As much as he missed the children, he liked his job here, although he sometimes chafed at wearing a suit and living by an alarm clock.

The Tiny Blessings agency was a good one, committed to doing Christ's work, though an ugly scandal had rocked the place over the last couple of years. Kelly, with her meticulous organizational skills had nearly killed herself to set things right. Or rather someone had tried to kill her to keep things quiet.

Thank God, the insane woman had been caught and dealt with. Kelly, Pilar and all the other staff members worked diligently, not only to move new adoptions forward, but to right the wrongs of the past.

But every time they doused one firestorm of trouble, another seemed to flame up. Someone still didn't want Kelly's husband, Ross, to investigate the old falsified adoption records and had recently sent a threatening letter to the agency.

As a newcomer, Eric often had trouble keeping up with events that had happened before he'd arrived. But he'd been blessed with a great new church and new friends, and was knee-deep in fund-raising efforts for his African projects. Life was good. Different but good.

Anne Williams, the agency's bookkeeper, appeared from the back of the long, narrow building. Eric liked the shy gentle woman, and he was glad she had married an old missionary acquaintance of his, Caleb Williams. In fact, Caleb, now a youth pastor, was the man who had recommended Eric for his current position.

A newspaper tucked beneath her arm, Anne said, "Andrew Noble called while you were conferencing with that new family."

Eric reached for the telephone. "Should I call him back?"

Anne shook her head. "He only wanted to thank you again for chairing the youth-group committee for the upcoming fund-raiser."

Every year the Noble Foundation held a picnic to raise funds for charitable groups. Eric was thrilled because this year the fund-raiser was earmarked for orphanages in Africa.

"Considering it's a project close to my heart, I'm glad to do it. And the kids at the youth center are full of ideas. A good bunch, too." He already knew most of them from his Sunday school class at the Chestnut Grove Community Church. Grabbing a pen, he scribbled a note to get snacks for tonight's meeting. Teens worked better when food was part of the deal. "Did Andrew mention if he or Rachel had found a cochair?"

The new international adoption program was taking a lot of his time. Add his already busy schedule, church and an occasional night out, and

Eric wasn't sure he could swing the full responsibility of organizing the youth's portion of the fund-
raiser. He hoped that Andrew and his cousin Rachel
would soon pick a cochair for the event.

"Andrew says Rachel has someone terrific in mind
and is awaiting a call back." Even though the
pregnant Rachel was on bed rest, she remained
involved with foundation work by telephone and
computer.

"Did he say who?" Not that it mattered. Eric would
work with anyone who desired to help his kids.

"You're going to like this." Anne placed the newspaper on the desk in front of him and tapped a
picture. "If Rachel can convince her, this is your
cochair."

Eric looked down at the newspaper photo. All the
air whooshed out of his lungs.

Samantha Harcourt. The woman he couldn't
forget even if he wanted to. The woman who dis-
turbed his dreams and whose memory sent waves of
humiliation flowing over him. He'd nearly made a
fool of himself in Africa. Had actually prayed for
God to send her back after that first amazing day.
Had spent many late nights standing outside the orphanage, listening to the call of the jackal, and
wishing he could forget her.

But how could he?

Now that he was back in the States, he found her
picture was literally everywhere. Billboards, magazines. Sam Harcourt, ad model for Style Fashions,
the hottest trend in America.

As a man who'd lived most of his adult life in Third World countries, he'd had no idea the sweet missions' worker was a top fashion model.

Once he'd discovered her identity, he'd felt like a total idiot. He'd also understood why she'd never returned to the orphanage. She wasn't a missions' worker at all. Like celebrities everywhere, she loved publicity and what better press than to say she'd worked among the poor, starving orphans of Africa?

Wasn't this photo proof enough? He remembered when she'd asked one of the kids to take it. She had both arms wrapped full of children, Matunde and Amani in her lap. The unfinished orphanage served as background.

A souvenir, she'd claimed. Yeah, right. Publicity, plain and simple.

He hissed in a slow, anxious breath.

Sam Harcourt was back in town.

Lord forgive him, but he prayed Sam would be too involved with herself to serve as his cochair.

Eric faked to the left, then bounded down the court, dribbling past two boys, both determined to slay him in their weekly game of Eric and the girls against the guys. Tonight was the first meeting of the picnic committee, but important things like basketball had to come first. He was ready to go up for the short jumper when the girls on his team suddenly gasped and stopped playing.

"It's her," Gina squeaked. "It's Samantha Harcourt."

Eric's heart stumbled. So did his feet. Sam was here.

He hoped that didn't mean what he thought it meant.

"Walk!" Caleb Williams blew his whistle, clapping his hands for the ball, but Eric forgot all about the game.

He stared at the entrance of the Youth Center. A tall, gorgeous blonde had come into the room, accompanied by her sister, a young mother Eric knew from church.

"I didn't know she was back in town," Gina gushed, eyes sparkling with admiration. Every teenager in the place was staring, drop-mouthed. Eric worked hard not to do the same.

Get it together, Pellegrino. You know what she really is. Another rich girl gone slumming.

Wasn't that what everyone back in his college days had said about Katrina before she'd dumped him for the country-club set? The same warning applied here.

"Is she going to help out in the center?" Nikki, another of the youth group, asked with that same sound of adulation.

Eric's lip curled, even while his traitorous heart slammed against his rib cage. "I think she's here for the meeting."

"No way," one of the kids said in hopeful disbelief.

"Way," he admitted, trying not to show his reluctance. "Rachel Cavanaugh asked her to work as my cochair."

He was not too happy about it, but he knew better than to say anything negative in front of a bunch of teenagers. In truth, he was ashamed of his negative reaction, but he'd been burned before. With Sam, he'd had no warning and she'd left her mark on him.

Gina, the shy, quiet one of the bunch, stared at Eric. "You know her?"

Though the rest of them were sweating like pigs, the slender teen wore a baggy sweater.

"Know her?" He shook his head. "Not really."

Which was perfectly true. The beautiful, compassionate woman he'd met in Africa clearly did not exist, and he felt like an idiot for building up this fantasy that she was his one and only, sent by God. Man, what a joke.

"If she helps with the fund-raiser, maybe we can get her to stick around here and help with other things." As youth director, Caleb was always on the lookout for more adult volunteers.

Eric stifled a protest. More time with Sam was the last thing he wanted. If he wasn't so committed to the work in Africa, he'd drop out of this fund-raiser himself.

"Maybe she'll start a fitness class," Gina said hopefully. "Models are usually great at staying in shape, and some of us need to work out more."

Eric found the remark amusing. Gina didn't have an ounce of fat on her.

"Whoa baby!" seventeen-year-old Jeremy murmured. "If Sam starts a class, I'm joining."

To everyone's amusement, Gina elbowed her boyfriend in the ribs.

When the nonsense died down, Caleb nudged Eric. "Are you going to welcome your helper?"

"Do I have to?" he asked and instantly regretted the reflexive response.

His friend shot him a strange look. Eric flushed, embarrassed to have Caleb see him so discombobulated. He needed to lope out the side door and get his head together.

"Eric," Sam called, the perfect smile lighting her face as she crossed the distance between them. "It really is you. I couldn't believe it when Rachel said we'd be working together again."

Eric's stomach sank to his toes. So, it was true. She *had* agreed to cochair. Dandy.

"Hello, Sam," he said coolly, mouth tight. "How's the modeling business?"

Samantha's smile faltered. She felt the chill of Eric's greeting clear to her bones. Disdain, cold and condemning filled his dark chocolate eyes, eyes that had followed her all over the world. But those same eyes that had once admired and welcomed her had grown icy. Her fear in Africa had been justified. Now that he knew who she was and what she did for a living, he didn't approve. She wasn't surprised, but she was disappointed.

"I'm sorry we didn't get a chance to say goodbye in Africa. Our shoot wrapped early and we had to catch a plane."

Her reasons, apparently, didn't impress him much. She tried again. "I've thought a lot about Africa since then."

"I'll bet you have."

Now what did he mean by that?

After one life-changing day at the orphanage with Eric, she'd thought of little else. She even dreamed about the profound despair and the selfless missionary with the teasing smile and the handsome face. Her life since that day had seemed empty and unfulfilling. Most people would think she was crazy, but with her career at its zenith, she'd come home to rethink her future. What did she want to do with the rest of her life?

"I'm on hiatus," she said, straightening her smile so that only she knew it was no longer real. Obviously, Eric wasn't as pleased to see her as she was to see him.

"That's nice." Eric glanced toward the clutch of gathered teenagers and motioned toward an open door. "Head for the meeting room, guys. Time to start planning."

And then he turned his back on her and walked away.

The next two hours were both miserable and wonderful for Sam. She liked the kids in the youth group. At first, they seemed intimidated or awed by her, something she hated. But after a bit, they opened up and began tossing out ideas in earnest, no longer focused on the celebrity in their midst.

Scribbling the latest brainstorm on a yellow pad, she glanced at Eric from the corner of her eye. He had not warmed up in the least. With the kids, he was friendly and funny just as he had been in Africa, but with her he was as cold as Antarctica. What had she

done, other than be who she was, to warrant his un-
friendliness?

"Let's see, we have nominations for a concession
stand, a space walk and pony rides. Does anyone know
where we could get ponies?" Eric pointed a pencil at
Caleb, who'd sat in on the meeting. "You know most
of the townsfolk better than I do. Any ideas?"

"I'll ask around and get back to you."

"We have to choose something simple that can be
put together easily but will still make plenty of
money," Sam said.

"The concession sounds easiest to me," Eric
answered. "We could make a schedule, work shifts,
assign different ones to collect the supplies." He
looked around the table. "What do the rest of you
think?"

"Sounds cool to me," Nikki answered. Of all the
teens, Goth girl Nikki was the most outspoken. "I'll
make the schedule of workers."

Several of the others groaned. Nikki was a tough
taskmaster.

"Is there any reason why we can't run two activities?" Sam asked as an idea hit.

All eyes turned to her, including Eric's dark
chocolate ones. "What do you have in mind?"

"How about a dunk tank?"

"Yes!" Jeremy said and punctuated his approval
with a fist in the air. "I can think of a million people
I'd pay to dunk. Starting with the school principal."

A chorus of excited voices pitched in, adding
opinions. Sam wrote them down as quickly as

possible, feeling pretty good to have come up with a popular possibility. When she glanced at Eric, he was watching her. She smiled. He didn't return it.

This voluntary position was going to be harder than she'd imagined.

After they had hashed out the initial ideas and responsibilities, Eric announced the next meeting date, then leaned back to gaze around the table. A cute smile danced at the corner of his lips. "Anybody hungry? I brought food."

With rumbles of approval and a clatter of chairs, the teenagers rushed the pile of snacks like a swarm of hungry locusts. Potato chips and cookies flew off the table while Eric handed out sodas from an ice chest. The man understood the language of kids, whether they were American or African.

"Thanks, Eric."

"Yeah, thanks, man."

The kids adjourned to the TV room and plopped down to eat. Sam found a diet soda and settled onto the floor beside the girl named Gina.

"Cold?" she asked.

Gina nodded and pulled a sweater closer to her narrow body.

"She's always cold," Jeremy answered as he slid down beside his girlfriend, paper plate piled high with food. Though he was tall and lanky, the brown-haired boy showed the muscular promise of coming manhood. He plunked a cookie and napkin in front of Gina. "Eat."

"I had supper."

"You did not." He waved the cookie under her nose. "I ate. You watched."

Gina turned her head away from the tempting chocolate sandwich. "My stomach's a little off today."

With a shrug, Jeremy placed the cookie on her knee and concentrated on demolishing his own plateful. Gina picked off a tiny corner of the cookie, then placed the remainder on her boyfriend's plate.

As Sam observed the exchange, a suspicion niggled at the back of her mind. After a bit, she shrugged it off. She didn't know these kids yet. Her concerns were likely the result of her own long struggle with food.

She sat quietly, getting to know the group by listening to their chatter. The lively talk reminded her of the days in junior high before food had taken control of her life. Other than Eric's odd behavior, tonight was fun and relaxing, a welcome respite from her hectic life.

Freckle-faced Tiffany obviously had a crush on Billy, but the shaggy-haired boy was clueless. Sam hid a smile when Tiffany took Billy's empty plate and Coke can, asking if he wanted anything else. Nikki, the Goth girl with kohl-rimmed eyes and black clothes, was the obvious leader. Young Dylan stayed on the perimeter, watchful and quiet.

Samantha wanted so badly to talk to Eric the way she had in Africa. How was he? Why was he here in Virginia? How were the boys, Matunde and Amani? She still treasured the single photo of them. She'd even had it blown up and framed to sit on her dresser—if the suite of rooms being remodeled at Harcourt Mansion was ever finished.

Soda can empty, she went to find a trash can.

"In the kitchen," Nikki called, guessing her intent.

The Youth Center had been built during Sam's long absence from Chestnut Grove and she was unfamiliar with the layout.

Rounding a corner, she slammed into the back of a broad-shouldered man. *Eric.*

He turned, his ready smile fading as soon as he recognized her. With a curt nod, he said, "Excuse me," and turned away again.

Sam caught his arm. The muscle beneath her hand tensed, rock hard.

"Eric, wait."

Reluctance hanging on him like a baggy shirt, he complied.

"Have I offended you in some way?" she asked quietly.

"Of course not. You've only just arrived."

"Then why the cold shoulder?"

Indecision came and went. Sam suspected he wanted to blow her off and escape. The honest man she'd met in Africa couldn't do that. "You should have told me who you were. It was a pretty big shock to come home to."

"Did it matter? Would you have treated me any differently?"

She saw the truth in his eyes. He would have. She would have been a fashion model, an object on display, instead of a person.

"You don't have to serve as cochair of this committee," he said. "I can find someone else or handle the job alone."

The words hurt. He neither needed nor wanted her. "You'd like me to quit?"

He hitched a shoulder. "I figure you're too busy for something like this. How did Rachel rope you into it?"

Sam didn't want to tell him, but she might as well. He'd find out soon enough. "She thought my involvement might be helpful."

"Helpful? In what way?"

Sam knew the minute he figured it out.

"Oh," he said. "I get it. People will come to see the famous model."

Trying not to bristle at the slight note of condescension, she squared her shoulders. "If using my name helps the kids, I'm willing to do it."

"Yeah," he said softly. "You're all about the kids, aren't you?"

His words weren't cruel but they cut just the same. And Sam knew as well as she knew the number of calories in a slice of bread that Eric didn't trust her goodwill one little bit.

Chapter Three

Sitting cross-legged on Ashley's pink duvet cover, Sam watched her sister gobble down three slices of thick pan double-cheese pizza and mentally calculated the calories and fat grams. To tell the truth, she couldn't remember the last time she'd tasted pizza but the smell was tantalizing. For most of her life, smelling pizza was as close as she dared come.

Following an afternoon around the family's magnificent backyard pool, she, Ashley and two-year-old Gabriel had come upstairs to Ashley's large bedroom suite to eat and talk, a sisterly act they hadn't embraced during their growing-up years. Funny how maturity and a little baby could change one's attitude.

Maturity had other effects, too. Or perhaps she could blame the perspective change on Africa. Her sister's living quarters included a private bathroom and balcony, as much space as the entire bedroom facility in Eric's orphanage.

In fact, the spectacular Harcourt Mansion, with seven bedrooms and nine bathrooms, was considerably larger than the space where thirty African children lived, slept and attended school.

The comparison made her feel guilty. Worse yet, her parents were renovating a huge area into a private apartment every bit as elegant as the best hotel, just for her.

"Have some pizza, Sam." Ashley pushed the opened box toward her.

Sam patted her empty stomach. "Not hungry."

Baby Gabriel, sitting on Sam's lap, reached for a slice. Ashley gently pushed his hand away and made a face. "I've been with you all day and you haven't eaten a bite. Eat. You're not going to lose your skinny-model body over a single piece of pizza."

Sam blinked, stunned. No wonder the pizza smell was killing her. She really *hadn't* eaten anything all day. Six years ago the monster of anorexia had sent her to the hospital, malnourished and dehydrated. Nobody, not even Ashley knew about her secret shame.

Since that frightening wake-up call and the subsequent months of treatment, she was regimented about her eating, making sure she took in sufficient nutrition every day. Somehow she'd gotten off schedule since coming back to Chestnut Grove.

With every ounce of willpower she possessed, Sam reached for a pizza slice. "Smells awesome."

Ashley chowed into a fourth slice. "Tastes even better."

Sam forced the pizza to her lips and took a bite. "Mmm. Delish."

The food lodged in the back of her throat. She grabbed her diet soda can and swigged, forcing the pizza down. During times like this, times of high stress or emotional unbalance, the anorexia tried to rear its murderous head. She'd done enough damage to her body already. Damage that might never heal. She couldn't allow the disorder to take control again. Next time, it might kill her.

"Why don't you come to church with us tomorrow, Sam?" Ashley asked as she handed LEGO blocks to her son with one hand and stuffed away pizza with the other.

"Chris is coming down after service."

Ashley's face glowed when she mentioned her fiancé, Chris Sullivan who pastored a church in Williamsburg. Some Sundays she and Gabriel drove up to spend the day with him. On others, he drove down to spend the afternoon with them. He was a great guy who'd helped Ashley forgive herself for past mistakes, and Sam was glad to finally see her sister so happy.

"The whole church thing seems weird to me."

"There's nothing weird about being a Christian."

"That's not what I meant." Since coming home, Sam had noticed a radical change in her family. Once cold and distant, her parents suddenly wanted to be close, to make up for lost time. They'd started attending church with Ashley and Gabriel and wanted Sam to do the same.

"I wish Mom and Dad had been this enthused about family when you and I were kids."

Gabriel threw a block onto the floor and laughed.

"Me, too, but if I learned anything through the ordeal with losing Gabriel and trying to get him back again, it's that we can't change the past. We have to move on, and try to do better in the future."

Ashley's teenage pregnancy had been a pivotal event for all of the Harcourts. Too afraid and ashamed to tell anyone, she'd given Gabriel up at first. When Sam had found out, she'd rushed home to help her sister regain custody of the baby. She couldn't imagine not having this precious boy in their lives.

Since then, Ashley was working hard to complete a degree in fashion design and looking forward to a future as Christopher's wife. She'd been lucky to find a man who not only didn't hold her past against her, but who loved her son as his own.

"I'm glad you found your path in life, sis. Really, I am. But church is so foreign to us Harcourts. All we've ever needed was money."

"Look what that got us." Ashley ripped off a piece of pizza, blew on it, then slid it into Gabriel's open mouth. Though the little guy had been well fed before the pizza had arrived, he responded with a toothy grin.

"Yeah. Reporters calling day and night to ask what we know about the adoption scandals. The whole town acts as if we personally stole babies and still have them hidden in the attic thirty years later."

They both laughed at the silliness. Gabriel patted the side of Sam's face with Bob the Builder. She caught his hand and kissed it, drawing in his clean baby smell as a powerful love welled up inside.

"I don't know why Grandfather falsified adoption papers and birth certificates. I wish I could understand. He hurt a lot of people."

"Money, Sam. Barnaby Harcourt was all about making money. That's all I remember about him. He looked like a kindly grandfather but he spent every waking moment getting richer."

"He could have made money by adopting out children honestly."

To the deep embarrassment of all the Harcourt family, Barnaby had extorted money from people who had given up their babies and then had spent years blackmailing them. Even the town mayor had fallen victim.

"Life has been insane around here since the construction workers found those papers in your wall," Ashley said.

"The Cavanaughs are nice people. Ben didn't deserve to find out about his birth parents that way."

Ironically, one of Ben's construction-company employees, Jonah Fraser, had discovered the hidden files. Since then, reporters had been hounding the Harcourt family, trying to blame them for Barnaby's misdeeds.

Hammering issued from the other end of the house.

"Funder," Gabriel said, eyes wide. For some reason, he'd developed a fear of thunder and lightning. Even though the hammering had continued off and on for weeks now, the toddler considered every sudden noise to be an ensuing storm.

"It's okay, sweetie," Sam crooned, raising the sturdy two-year-old body up to her shoulder.

"Someday they will actually finish those rooms and stop hammering."

Ashley chuckled. "And about the time they have the entire suite just the way you want it, you'll run back to Chicago."

"I don't think so. I'm thinking of renting out my condo."

"Are you serious?" Ashley's face registered disbelief. "Why?"

"I'm not sure I want to go back to modeling." Even while she was on hiatus, the pressure never stopped. Only today her agent had called, urging her to get back to Chicago. "Not full-time anyway."

The idea horrified her sister. "Are you crazy? Why wouldn't anyone want your life?"

"Africa," she said simply.

Ashley titled her head, puzzled. "Now that makes perfect sense. Care to elaborate?"

Sam shrugged. "Africa did something to me, Ash. Poverty like I can't even express and yet the people have this joy, this strength about them."

"Excuse me if I have no clue what this has to do with your amazing career."

"Everything." Gabriel wiggled to be let down, so Sam turned him loose. He scooted toward the edge of the bed. "I want my life to matter more. I want to make a difference. Standing in front of a camera in pretty clothes seems so empty after what I saw there."

"Well, half the female population would take your place in a heartbeat if they could."

Sam knew it was true. She also knew a lot of things about the business her sister didn't. Sure, hers was a great job, but money and success in modeling came with a high price. A price she wouldn't share with anyone, even her baby sister.

She fiddled with the edge of the pizza box, tempted to have another slice. "What do you think of Eric Pellegrino?"

"He's a hunk and a half. Almost as cute as my Chris. A nice guy, too. Everyone at church seems to like him." Ashley poked a finger at Sam's knee. "Why? What does Eric have to do with our conversation?"

"We met in Africa."

Ashley's mouth formed an O. "No kidding?"

Gabriel turned onto his belly and started to slide off the high bed feetfirst. Without breaking the line of conversation, Ashley helped him safely down. He toddled to his push pony and climbed aboard, saying, "Horsey, go."

"I worked at Eric's orphanage for a day," Sam said. "It was like nothing I've ever experienced. I found myself wishing I could stay there forever."

"You? In an African orphanage? With dirt and flies and poverty? And no beauty salon?"

Sam gave a self-deprecating laugh. "Yes. How weird is that?"

She told her sister the rest, about the children, the lack of food, the despair. Most of all, she talked about Eric.

When she finished, Ashley's soft brown eyes danced with speculation. "Are you in love with this guy?"

Sam made a face to quell a sudden invasion of nervous butterflies. "I barely know him. And now that we've met again, I think he hates me."

"Oh, come on, Sam. There is not a red-blooded male in this country who hates you."

"Then let's say he doesn't like me much. He holds me at an arm's length and when I try to talk to him, he's as cool as a Frappuccino."

Ashley grinned. Having found her own true love, Ashley saw romance everywhere. "I think you're way off base. Maybe the guy likes you a lot. And maybe he's intimidated because you're famous and he's just a missionary."

"Eric Pellegrino is not *just* a missionary. Nor is he intimidated by anything. He seems to despise what I do. And maybe he should. He's dedicated to a noble cause. I'm dedicated to shopping and accessorizing."

"Yes, but you're so good at it!"

They both laughed, but Sam wasn't joking. Along with her desire to change her own life, she wanted to change Eric's opinion of her. She just didn't know how.

When Eric walked into the Youth Center arts-and-crafts room, the first person he spotted was Samantha. Like radar, he seemed to find her. It was maddening. Yesterday, he'd spotted her going into the Noble Foundation. The day before, he'd driven past the mall and amidst all the cars and people, he'd seen Sam.

Now, here he was, that funny feeling in his gut, watching her with the teens. She and the girls, plus

Anne Williams, were hub deep in conversation about hairstyles of all things. The boys sat at the table, chins on hands, looking bored to the point of coma.

Tiffany had brought a fashion magazine and was pointing to a picture. Sam placed a finger on each of the girl's cheekbones, indicated the shape of her face and said something that made the slightly pudgy girl smile.

Eric had to give Sam that much. She was kind to the kids although they still treated her with a star-struck adulation that set his teeth on edge. She was only a person. No better than the rest of them.

He felt in the back pocket of his jeans for the letter that had arrived today.

"Hey, guys," he called to the dying-of-boredom boys. They whirled as if he'd saved them from a fate worse than death. Chuckling, he understood all too well. To a guy, discussing girls' hairstyles *was* pretty deadly.

"What's up, Eric?" Lanky Jeremy scraped a chair out from the table to make room for their leader.

"Got some news today." He unfolded the letter and placed it on the table. "From Africa."

Sam, who had been describing some bizarre thing called *shine serum,* stopped in mid-sentence and looked up at him. He hadn't intended to notice her at all tonight and yet, here he was soaking in the way sprigs of blond hair framed her face and brought out the beauty in her gray eyes.

"Africa?" she asked, tone eager. "From your or-phanage?"

Technically it wasn't his orphanage anymore though he'd founded and built the place. The missions' board was in charge. "From the boys I'm trying to adopt."

Three of the teenagers in the group had been adopted. Those three always wanted up-to-the-minute details on Eric's process to adopt Matunde and Amani. They huddled around his back, staring down at the letter. Telephone or Internet contact with the new director was spotty at best, so every time he received a letter from the boys, he was pumped for days.

To his surprise, Sam rose, too, and came around to his side of the table. "Matunde and Amani?"

His surprise doubled. "You remember them?"

"Of course I do. I have a picture of them that I treasure."

"Oh, right." The photo she used for publicity. That was why she remembered his boys.

Sam pressed in beside him, leaning onto the table to read the letter along with the others. Right at his elbow, she brought with her the luscious scent of some perfume that probably cost enough to fund the orphanage for a year. And as annoyed as he tried to be about that, his senses couldn't help appreciating the warm, feminine fragrance or the way her slender arm grazed the side of his.

"Did you say you're adopting them?" Sam asked, turning her head so that their faces were only inches apart.

A hitch in his chest, Eric was trapped between Sam, the table and a huddle of kids. He couldn't escape if he wanted to—and he most definitely wanted to. Yes, indeed. He needed to get far away from Miss Rich and Famous.

"Trying to. International adoptions are long and complex. The rules change constantly."

"So what are the rules saying right now? Can you or can you not bring the boys to America?"

She seemed genuinely interested, just as she had in Africa. Why was it that the Sam he talked to was not the Sam he knew her to be?

"The government officials who will make the decision know me, at least by reputation. They're the same people I'm working with to develop the new African adoption program for Tiny Blessings."

"So, when are the boys coming?"

"I don't know. These things take time."

"But why? They're orphans, alone in the world. You love them. They should just get on an airplane and come." She dragged out the chair beside him and sat down, turning to prop a fist on her beautiful cheekbone.

His pulse, already misbehaving, skittered dangerously.

Eric looked around and realized that the kids had moved away. A clutch of girls shot sly glances at him. One giggled when he caught her staring.

What was that all about?

Bewildered, he returned his attention to Sam's question. "If all goes well, I'm shooting for Christmas."

"Nothing will go wrong. You'll get them. You and the boys are going to have the best Christmas ever."

He wanted that with all his heart. Nothing could go wrong. He'd promised their father to care for them. He loved them. They loved him. Everything would work out. It had to.

"You'll be a wonderful father, Eric." Sam spontaneously pressed a hand over the top of his. Little jolts of electricity shot all the way up to his shoulder. "I saw you with them. You already are."

Eric tried to remember why Sam Harcourt turned him cold, but with her sweet eyes looking at him this way and their hands touching, his mind was blitzed.

"Hey, you two. Any chance we can have a meeting tonight? Or is this a private party?" Caleb Williams ambled toward them, his wife Anne at his side. Their smiles had Eric wondering. Did they think there was something going on between him and Sam?

Man, were they ever confused.

"Time to get started, I guess." By sheer force of will he got up and moved to the head of the table, leaving Sam where she was. Instantly, his vacant chair was filled by one of the girls and the chitchat began about Nikki's haircut. Should she get a skunk stripe or not?

Eric was hard-pressed not to laugh but he noticed Sam took the question with complete seriousness.

He called the meeting to order and was pleased that the kids had followed through with their assignments. Very quickly, he collected price lists, tentative work schedules, booth ideas and a host of other details the kids had come up with on their own.

"We'll need a full workday before the picnic," he said. "To set up booths, put up signs, decorate."

"What about the day before?"

"Can't," he said. "My calendar is full. I have to work."

"I don't," Sam said. "The kids and I can handle it."

With school still weeks away, most of the kids were at loose ends. So was Sam. Eric's lip curled. She was on *hiatus,* a word the rest of the world barely understood.

"All right. Sounds good to me. I'll leave the particulars up to you."

Gina, usually quiet as a mouse, piped up. "Maybe the two of you should get together that night and go over everything. I mean, Eric can't be there Friday. Sam needs to fill him in on the plans."

"Great idea," Nikki added. "Don't you think, guys?" She gave the other teens a look that said they'd better agree and do it fast.

"Yeah. Sure. Eric, you don't want to be in the dark. No telling what we might do without your input. You can't trust a bunch of teenagers, you know. You and Sam should definitely get together that last Friday night before the picnic."

Why were the kids behaving so strangely? He glanced at Sam, saw a flush on the crest of her cheekbones. He looked at Caleb and then at Anne. They both grinned like African hyenas.

What was up with this?

"All right. Sure. Whatever." He looked at Sam. "Is that okay with you?"

She nodded mutely, an unusual turn of events, and Eric adjourned the meeting to the dining room.

As he pushed back from the table, Caleb came toward him, that annoying grin still on his face. "Might as well give up."

"What are you talking about?" All these undercurrents were making him grumpy.

"The kids. They did it to Anne and me."

Eric got a bad feeling. "Did what?"

"Played matchmaker."

"And?"

"And now they have their sights set on you and Sam."

"Me? Sam?" His blood pressure shot up. "You're losing it, brother."

At Caleb's soft chuckle, Eric's belly went south. He was having enough trouble with his own head on the subject of Samantha Harcourt. If this bunch of teenagers started in, he'd have no peace at all. Samantha was not the kind of woman he wanted to be interested in. Women like her aimed for the kneecaps and left you alone and bleeding.

At the sound of giggling, Eric glanced toward the dining-room doorway. Three pairs of teenaged eyes gleamed at him with speculation.

He was in trouble here. Serious trouble.

Chapter Four

Sam gazed around at the group of kids once again gathered in the Youth Center. They worked in small groups, sipping Cokes and munching on the tray of melon she had provided. A few lettered signs and glittered banners while others organized lists of volunteers and donations for the various booths. They were a good team with minimal arguments. Although a few heated discussions had cropped up in their days of working together, the problems were easily resolved.

Thank goodness this was one of the last committee meetings before the picnic. Not that she didn't like the kids or enjoy the work. It wasn't that at all. In fact, she'd taken on the task of helping Andrew Noble with some of the advance publicity for the event and found a certain satisfaction in both tasks. If her agent would stop calling every hour she'd almost be content.

The problem with the youth group was Eric. Or rather, the teens' matchmaking attempts between Eric and her. Just when he'd begun to warm up a little, the kids had come up with this ridiculously obvious scheme and made them both uncomfortable.

From her spot next to Gina, she slid a look in Eric's direction. He, Caleb, Jeremy and a couple of the other boys hammered together the wooden frame for the concession booth.

The muscles in his athletic shoulders flexed with each hammer strike, reminding her of that day in Africa. Even in ordinary jeans and a yellow T-shirt that darkened his skin to bronze, Eric was by far the best-looking guy in Chestnut Grove. At least from her viewpoint.

He was nothing like most men of her acquaintance, but that was a good thing. Deep inside, Sam remained a small-town girl who admired a man with the common sense to change his own tires and wield a hammer. A man's man. Masculine, strong, steady.

Gina's voice interrupted her ruminations. "He's cute for an older guy."

Great, she'd been caught staring. "When are all of you going to give this up? Neither Eric nor I are interested."

"Really?" Nikki asked, popping a square of juicy watermelon past her black-lined lips. She clearly didn't believe Sam's protest.

"Really. Now can we talk about something else?"

"Well, we do have another idea," Gina said.

"Oh, good." Sam rolled her eyes heavenward. "Now I'm really worried."

"We want to know how you keep in shape."

That question she could handle. She sprinkled glitter around a block letter and said, "I have a daily exercise regime, which I never skip." Style would fire her in a New York minute unless she looked perfect in their clothes. "Why?"

She worked like crazy to stay in shape and worried constantly. Between the need to properly handle her eating disorder and the need to stay in perfect condition, she often felt as though she would never be enough. Not good enough. Not pretty enough. Not thin enough.

That feeling was part of the vicious cycle that had caused the disorder in the first place.

"We want you to start a workout program here at the center for us." Gina pushed her paper plate of melon to one side. After cutting a single slice of cantaloupe into a dozen tiny bites, she'd left it mostly uneaten. A warning bell, one that had rung every time she'd been with Gina, went off in Sam's head.

"You don't need an exercise program," Sam said earnestly.

"Gina doesn't. She has great willpower, but the rest of us can't stay away the French fries. Won't exercise offset the calories?" Tiffany asked hopefully.

"That all depends, but exercise helps. You need exercise anyway," Sam said. "The most important thing is maintaining good health."

"You sound like my mom," Tiffany said.

"Sorry. But your mom is right. Your health is everything." Sam had learned that the hard way. Some things lost could never be regained.

"So will you do it?" Nikki pressed. "Will you start a class?"

She worked out anyway. Why not encourage the girls to stay fit in the process? Exercising with them would be a lot more fun than doing it alone. "I could ask Scott if the church would mind. It's easy to set up a combination Jazzercise/aerobics regime. It might even be fun."

And in the process she could discuss healthy eating with the girls and get better acquainted with Gina. The girl worried her.

"We could meet here." Tiffany's round face was excited. A green marker in hand, she pointed around the Youth Center. "There's plenty of room. And I would so love to go back to school this fall with a new, slimmer body."

"Well, I'm a slave driver, let me warn you."

Nikki grinned, the black lipstick a startling contrast to her white teeth. "We're tough. We can take it."

"Okay, then," Sam replied, shaking loose glitter onto a clean piece of paper. "I'll check with Caleb to be sure it's okay. Maybe I could help you get started before I return to work."

"Planning on leaving soon?" a masculine voice asked. Eric popped open a cold Coke and took a long drink, his eyes watching her over the rim.

"Sam's going to start an aerobics class for us,"

Nikki said. She slid another bite of melon into her mouth and smiled around it.

"Maybe." Sam softened the reminder with a smile. "I said I'd check into it."

"Nice of you, but if you're headed back to Chicago, how can you do that?"

Sam shrugged. "I don't have any set agenda at the moment except for a few things I can fly to and be back in a couple of days."

Never mind that the agency was hounding her to do more public appearances for Style. But even the gig to hand out an award at some Hollywood awards program couldn't tempt her to leave Chestnut Grove right now. Maybe she was burned out.

Eric scraped a chair away from the table and straddled it, leaning both arms on the back. The Coke can dangled from his strong, masculine fingertips. "Eventually, though, you'll go back to Chicago."

He seemed almost insistent.

"I haven't decided yet exactly what I'm going to do."

"What do you want to do?"

The question, much like something he would have said in Africa, surprised her.

"I'm reevaluating." She wasn't sure how much to tell him. Sometimes when they talked, he seemed genuinely interested. At others, he appeared to be judging every word and finding her unworthy.

"What's to reevaluate? You have a great career that pays well. You get to travel all over the world. People know your face."

"Sometimes that's not a good thing."

"Poor little rich girl?" he asked.

She studied his expression to see if he was making fun of her. He wasn't.

"It's not that. It's having people make assumptions about me because of what I do for a living."

The answer caught him off guard. He waited two beats before smile lines crinkled around his eyes. "I think you just took me down a notch."

"Not intentionally. I'm an average person, Eric. Not a face. Not a celebrity. Just a person." She capped the red glitter with a snap and reached for the blue. "How's the booth coming?"

"Almost finished." He motioned toward the structure with his Coke can. "Do you think we should paint it or leave it raw?"

Sam looked toward the girls for their opinion. "What do you think, ladies? Paint or not?"

The girls exchanged looks and Sam tried not to sigh in exasperation. Every time she and Eric spoke, the teens started up again. Before anyone could answer, a scrawny, hawk-nosed man entered the room.

Sam tensed. Her interior decorator. Why was he here? She thought they had everything settled with remodeling her suite.

"Miss Harcourt." In his usual fit of hyperactivity, the man rushed to her. "I need your opinion."

"At this time of night? Really, Dennis, you work too hard. You should go home and relax."

"It simply cannot wait until tomorrow. I'll be up

all night fretting if we wait. When you left this afternoon, I was all aflutter, worrying what to do."

Sam stifled a sigh. The decorator with his finicky ways and temperamental demands was wearing thin. Trying her best to remain positive and polite, she asked, "What's wrong this time?"

Drawing up in a stiff, pigeon-chested stance, Dennis sniffed. "You know, of course, that I've designed rooms for other well-known clients. When I did the Manhattan suite for JLo, she gave me complete carte blanche."

Sam longed to crawl under the table. The last thing she wanted was for Dennis to name drop in front of Eric and the kids. Her parents had hired the decorator as a gift to her, but sometimes she wished she had done the job herself. More than that, she wished she could cancel the entire renovation. She hadn't wanted or needed the expensive work.

Dennis tossed his hands into the air. "I can't work under these conditions."

Sam glanced around at the group of fascinated teens and then at Eric. He seemed to be studying his sweating Coke can with unusual interest.

"Exactly what can I help you with, Dennis?"

"Your carpenter, that Jonah Fraser fellow, painted the east wall of the sitting room today. It's blue. Robin's-egg blue, a shade that simply will not work behind your mask collection."

Oh, please.

Sam counted to ten before answering. In her business she worked with finicky people all the time.

A people pleaser, she wanted to make all of them happy.

"I know you want perfection, Dennis, and the rooms are coming together beautifully, but the paint Jonah used is the color you and I chose last week."

"It doesn't work. We have to get something else. You'll hate it and my reputation will be ruined. Ruined, I say."

Sam rose from her chair and gently guided Dennis toward the exit. She could feel Eric's gaze on her back.

"Everything will be fine, Dennis. I'm sure with your exceptional creative talent, you'll think of a way to make all the elements blend together. That's why we hired you. Your reputation for turning the ordinary into the magnificent is impeccable."

He simpered. "You're right. I can do this. I can make the ugliest room into a showplace. Thank you, Miss Harcourt." He grabbed her hand and squeezed. "I knew you'd understand. Should I order those plants we discussed this morning?"

"You do that. And I'll see you tomorrow. Okay?" She pushed him out the door with a wave and turned back toward the room.

"Gee, Sam, you have an interior designer all the way from New York?" Tiffany asked in awe.

"He's good at his job. Just a little sensitive."

Sneaking a peek at Eric, she saw him watching her. What was he thinking? That she really was pretentious and shallow? That only a completely self-absorbed woman would hire an interior designer when children in Africa drank from mud holes?

The familiar ache pushed at her rib cage.

Maybe Eric was right. Maybe she was as superficial as he seemed to think.

For the next hour and a half, Sam tried to shake off the negative feelings by throwing all her energy into the project. Hands covered in glitter, she headed for the ladies' room to wash up.

Once inside, she heard retching. Someone was sick.

"Who's in here?" she asked.

"Me."

"Gina? What's wrong?"

"I'm okay."

Sam stood against the wall, holding her breath, hoping she was wrong and wondering what to do if she was right.

After a couple of minutes, the stall lock clicked and Gina came out, as pale as Liquid Paper.

"You look sick, Gina. What's the matter?"

The girl splashed cold water on her face. "Something I ate, I guess. The burger was kind of greasy."

"Are you sure that's all?" Sam's nerves jangled with warning. Something was not right with this girl and she suspected an eating disorder. Whenever the group met, everyone else ate like starving dogs. Gina usually picked at her food, but tonight her boyfriend had brought in a burger and insisted she eat it.

"I'm not pregnant if that's what you mean."

"It's not what I meant. But I'm glad to know you aren't. That's a complication you don't need at your age."

Gina looked at her, then looked away quickly, as if she wanted to open up but was too scared. Sam knew the feeling.

"Have you been dieting?" She tried to sound casual, knowing how deceptive and secretive an anorexic could be.

"I'm okay, Sam. Really. Stop worrying." Gina spun away from the mirror and pasted on a smile. "See. I'm fine now. That greasy burger. That's what did it."

Then Gina hurried out of the restroom, leaving Sam to follow. Someone who Gina knew and trusted needed to talk to her.

"Obviously not me," Sam muttered as she pushed the door open and stepped into the hallway.

Wrestling with what to do, she saw Gina back with the group, laughing at Eric. Someone had stuck a child's birthday hat on his head, complete with a rubber band indenting his chin, and he pretended not to notice. The sight of the big, strong man pounding nails while wearing a birthday hat made her laugh, too.

Eric. The kids liked and trusted him. He was their leader here and knew the people of the church much better than she did. Maybe he'd know what to do about Gina.

"Eric," she said. "Could I talk to you in private?"

He laid aside the hammer. "Sure."

"Oooh, Eric," one of the boys teased. "She wants to talk in private."

Eric tossed the birthday hat at him. "Go paint something, Dylan."

The boy and his buddies laughed. Sam tried her best to ignore their not-so-subtle innuendo as she led the way out of the center into the warm August evening. When she was certain they were no longer in earshot, she rested her back against the brick wall and told him her concerns about Gina.

Darkness had come and the pulse of cicadas served as musical backdrop to the quiet conversation.

Eric listened intently, his face dimly visible by the security lights. "You think Gina has some kind of eating disorder?"

"I do. And after she was sick a few minutes ago, I think my suspicion bears checking out."

"She looked okay to me. Did you ask her what was wrong?"

"She said it was the greasy burger."

"Too much grease *can* make a person sick."

"Eric, haven't you noticed how thin she is?"

"You're thin."

Sam didn't go there. "I've always been thin."

"So has she."

Exasperated, she tried another angle. "A skinny teenager shouldn't be counting the calories in a piece of watermelon. I heard her do that tonight."

"This is out of my league, Sam. But just because she's thin and had an upset stomach is no reason to put ideas into her head about anorexia. Sometimes I wonder if that's how stuff like this gets started."

"I'm not trying to put ideas into her head. She could already be in serious trouble." She perched both hands on her hips and look skyward, scared to say too much but wanting him to realize the seriousness of her claim. "I've known models with eating disorders, Eric. I know what I'm talking about."

"Are you sure you're not overreacting because of that?" Silhouetted against the building, hands shoved into his back pockets, he looked mysterious and attractive.

Sam huffed out an annoyed sound. Why had she thought a man would understand?

"I thought she might listen to you or that you might know a counselor or someone that could help. But apparently I was wrong. Excuse me for bothering you with this."

Feeling like a hysterical female, she shoved away from the wall and left him standing in the dark.

Chapter Five

"Anyone involved with Tiny Blessings could potentially be in danger."

Ross Van Zandt tossed the latest edition of the *Richmond Gazette* onto Eric's desk. Every inch a former New York cop, the private investigator's usual wary expression was even more intense today.

"If you're worried about Kelly," Eric said, "I'll keep an eye out when she's here."

He already did. With all the troubling undercurrents and two pregnant co-workers, he was taking no chances.

"After the threatening note Kelly received on the Fourth of July, I'm worried about everyone." Ross offered a crooked smile. "Maybe a little more about Kelly since she's my pregnant wife." He tapped the letter to the editor. "Whoever we've upset by reopening all these old adoption cases is getting more agitated by the day. This latest demand for Jared to stop writing articles about the investigation is vehement."

Eric scanned the scathing letter. "No kidding. Do you think we need to hire a security guard for the agency?"

"I've talked to Kelly about that, but she's adamant. To her way of thinking, if we hire security or display a police presence, prospective parents will be afraid to come here."

"She has a point. Kelly works hard to make the place inviting and comfortable for the families and the women who trust us to find homes for their babies."

Besides the well-appointed rooms where adoptive parents relaxed on plush sofas and had refreshments while taking parenting classes, the agency provided a playground in back for foster kids in their program. The walls were lined with happy photos of children who had been adopted through the agency over the years. Kelly's office even boasted a fireplace for those chilly winter days when a fire and hot cocoa made life seem a little brighter. The old building had intentionally been decorated to relax and reassure.

"I urged the Harcourt family to be alert, as well," Ross said. "They have a good security system already in place but since we don't know who we're dealing with, we can't be certain that's enough."

Eric rose from his desk and went to the window. The mention of anything concerning Sam made him jumpy. Last night he'd upset her and today he couldn't get her out of his head. Ah, what was he thinking? He'd had Samantha in his head for over a year.

"I'm not sure why anyone would be worried about the Harcourts. Their part in this is long past."

"That old mansion holds a lot of secrets, Eric. Maybe someone is afraid more will be uncovered."

"Like Ben's forged adoption records?" Eric asked softly.

Out on the playground beyond the patio, a swing moved gently in the summer breeze, a reminder that this building was about children. Forgeries and attempted murder seemed so out of place. Lately, he worried the agency's problems would wing their way across the ocean and cause problems. Problems neither he, Matunde nor Amani needed right now. At those times, he questioned his decision to come here. Daily he prayed that nothing happened to stop the adoption of his boys.

"If one wall of the house secreted documents," Ross said, "others could, too. The Harcourts need to be aware they might be sitting on a powder keg."

Having never considered that Samantha might be in danger, Eric wondered why she didn't go back to Chicago where she belonged. She claimed to be reevaluating, whatever that meant. But small, provincial Chestnut Grove held nothing for a woman like her.

"The Harcourts are nearly finished with the remodeling," he said, turning to prop a hip on the windowsill. "But short of tearing the house down, how could anyone find out what else Barnaby might have hidden there?"

Ross took a stress ball from Eric's desk and tossed it back and forth between his palms. "Lindsay

Morrow would have burned the place if she thought she could conceal the truth about her husband's indiscretions. Whoever wants things kept quiet this go-round could be just as demented."

The issue with the mayor and his mentally deranged wife had happened more than a year before Eric had moved to Chestnut Grove. But Eric had been apprised of the former problems. Problems that wouldn't go away even though Lindsay Morrow was now institutionalized.

Someone was still very determined to protect a long-ago secret.

An idea flitted through Eric's head. Sam's family was the original cause of the problems. Wouldn't they have more to hide than anyone?

"What about someone in the Harcourt family?" he asked, reaching out to catch the stress ball in mid-toss. "Could they be involved in the cover-up?"

Ross thought about the question, weighing his answer like a good cop. "I don't think so. This whole thing has them pretty shaken and Sam certainly wouldn't want all this extra publicity. She came home for a break. Not to say we shouldn't be alert to any possibility. A lot of adoptions went through this agency during the corrupt reign of Barnaby Harcourt."

He held out his hand for the stress ball. Eric tossed it to him.

"Are you saying more than one person may want to keep the past buried?" Now *that* was a scary thought. Dealing with one sicko was bad enough.

"Possibly." Ross tapped the spongy ball against his stubbled chin. "I lose sleep at night trying to figure this thing out. Some people will go to extremes when threatened. I was there the night Lindsay tried to kill Kelly. It was the most terrifying moment of my life."

Eric had seen the steely-eyed detective turn to mush in the company of his wife. He had no doubt Ross would have taken a bullet for Kelly if necessary.

"Thank God no one was killed."

"You got that right, buddy. I thank God every single day that we all came out of there alive." Ross picked up the file he'd come for and started toward the door. "I don't want things to get that crazy this time. We have to figure out whose cage we've rattled. The sooner, the better."

"Anything I can do to help?"

"Be alert and pray a lot." With a grin, Ross tossed the stress ball. Eric one-handed it. "Other than that, we have to wait for this person to either act or reveal his identity."

The notion of waiting for a nut to crack was about as comforting as sleeping with a python.

His intercom buzzed and a teenage volunteer reminded Eric of a four o'clock appointment.

"Sorry to run out on you, Ross, but I have a meeting with Rachel Cavanaugh."

Ross frowned. "I thought Rachel was on bed rest until her baby comes."

"She is, but apparently the woman can't be stopped from working on Noble Foundation causes from her bedroom."

"Eli must be going crazy about that."

"She's lucky to have a doctor for a husband."

"Yeah." Ross laughed. "If only she'd pay attention to him. Tell her I said hello."

He executed a jaunty salute and disappeared down the hall toward the records room.

On the way to his meeting with Rachel, Eric tried to shake off the worries Ross had dropped on his desk. In Africa he'd dealt with tribal tensions, wild animals and limited water supplies. If Tiny Blessings' staff were in danger, as the primary male employee, he'd have to keep his eyes and ears open.

Ross was right about one thing. He needed to pray a lot.

At the door of the charming older brick colonial the Cavanaughs called home, Eric was met by a scrub-clad nurse.

"Rachel's holding court in the living room," the young woman said, showing Eric into a beautifully restored room with wide-plank flooring and dentil molding. The rest of the house appeared to be in a state of progress. Eric liked the cozy feel instantly.

"Don't keep her too long," the nurse instructed. "Even though she protests, she tires easily." She shot an affectionate look at her charge.

Rachel smiled back. "Thanks, Shelby. Would you mind bringing my guest something to drink?"

Eric waved her off. "Nothing for me, thanks."

The young nurse smiled and disappeared, taking a pair of empty glasses and a magazine with her.

Eric seated himself. "How are you doing, Rachel?"

He and the Cavanaughs attended the same church and through additional work with the foundation had developed a budding friendship. Rachel came from a wealthy family, something that normally set his teeth on edge, but the Nobles used their money for good, unlike most of the rich folks he'd encountered.

"As you can well see, I am a fat but very happy woman. If only this little Cavanaugh were not quite so fussy at times."

"What do the doctors say?"

"Well, Dr. Daddy doesn't want me to move, much less work. But my OB doctors have approved a few hours a day from this spot as long as I take it easy. Believe me, I am taking it so easy I could scream."

The picture of cool elegance even in her advanced state of pregnancy, Rachel had developed a simple system to keep her finger in the pies at the Noble Foundation. A laptop and a conference telephone were within arm's reach without having to leave her bed. When she'd phoned Eric yesterday, her voice had held a hint of excitement.

Eric figured he could use a little good news.

"You're on our prayer list at the agency." Every morning the staff met for updates and prayer. They kept a running list of friends and situations that needed the Lord's special touch.

"I appreciate that. And I have full confidence that the baby and I both will come through this preeclampsia thing with flying colors." She shifted her very round body and asked, "So how's your picnic committee coming along?"

At the reminder of the committee, Eric thought of Sam again. A knot formed in his belly. He still wondered why she'd come to him about Gina. He knew nothing about such things, but he couldn't imagine a sweet Christian girl like Gina being so foolish. All teenage girls, he supposed, worried about their weight. His sisters had. They'd even gone on crazy fad diets a few times, but none of them had starved themselves to death. Didn't that only happen in made-for-TV movies?

Well, whatever, Sam was annoyed with him. He didn't like that. Not because it was Sam but because he didn't like tension and trouble with anyone.

And now that the teens were playing their silly matchmaking game, he was really uncomfortable. How did he tell the kids, in a Christian manner, that Sam's lifestyle and his did not mesh?

"Sam and the kids are working on the last-minute preparations today."

And tonight he and Sam had a private meeting at the Starlight Diner to go over the end result. He still couldn't figure out how that had happened. He shook his head. Teenagers. He'd been safer in the jungles of Africa.

"For the past three days my telephone at home and at the office have rung continually. The kids are all over this project with great enthusiasm."

Rachel picked the silky ruffle on a throw pillow. "How are things working out with you and Sam?"

"Excuse me?"

Rachel laughed. "I meant with Sam as your cochair."

Given the matchmaking thoughts streaming through his head, Eric was glad his skin was too dark to blush. "Fine."

"Excellent. I knew she'd be great. Besides her obvious clout, Sam Harcourt is not afraid of hard work."

He'd thought the same thing in Africa, but here he wasn't so sure. Standing in front of a camera or discussing color swatches with her decorator wasn't Eric's idea of work. But, he had to admit she never missed a meeting with the committee and had carried her share of the load.

"I think everything is about ready with the other committees, too," Rachel went on. "Andrew has worked hard, adding in these fresh ideas. I hate to miss it, but if the weather cooperates, we should have an excellent fund-raiser even without me there."

"I hope so," Eric answered, glad to be off the topic of Samantha. "Africa is a worthy charity."

A smug smile crossed Rachel's pretty face. "Africa is exactly why I've asked you to come by. And not just because of the picnic. I have some very exciting news."

Right now the most exciting news Eric wanted was word that Matunde and Amani could be adopted. The African government was balking for reasons they had yet to explain.

Rachel pointed to an elegant burgundy briefcase

next to an end table. "Would you get that for me please? I feel like such a helpless ninny, but I don't dare bend or lift even something that small."

"Not a problem." Eric did as he was asked, placing the valise on the table next to her. She clicked it open.

"This has been in the works for a while, and I've been excited to share it with you, but we just now have the particulars ironed out." She lifted out a folder. "Someone has made a substantial donation to the Noble Foundation to sponsor an orphanage in Africa. I thought, since you have the most experience in that realm, I would ask your help in deciding which one."

Eric leaned back in the plush chair, pulse kick-starting. "Are you serious?"

"Absolutely."

Now, this was something that raced his engine. "There are so many facilities that could use the help, but I'm partial to the baby hospital and Ithemba House. I've worked in and with both. They're entirely donor funded and do an exceptional job with limited resources."

Very limited.

"Isn't Ithemba the orphanage you founded?"

Eric blinked. "How did you know that?"

Rachel gave a tiny smile. "I have my sources." She removed a paper and handed it to him. "Will this sum be useful?"

Eric stared down at the amount. His mouth went as dry as dust. "Is this a joke?"

"I never joke about foundation funding."

Excitement warmed his blood as possibilities streamed through his head. He couldn't believe this.

"That's not only enough to fund the basic needs for a year, we could even buy some new medical equipment for the baby hospital. The X-ray machine is a pitiful antique."

A slow smile lifted from Rachel's lips to her eyes. "I was hoping you'd say that. Will you serve as adviser on the project?"

"I'd be honored." More than honored, he was floored. Someone had just donated enough money to make a difference for a lot of children.

"Who's the donor? I want to send him a personal thank you."

"The donor asks to remain anonymous."

So it was an individual, not a corporation. One single person with money had stepped up to the plate. "Tell him, he's my new hero. I've prayed for something like this for years."

"Well, my friend." Rachel's smile became Cheshire-like. "Sometimes God works in mysterious ways."

Eric was so thrilled with the donation that he didn't wonder about Rachel's cryptic remark until much later.

Samantha strapped her baby nephew Gabriel into a high chair at the Starlight Diner and pulled it against the table's edge to wait for Eric.

Ever since she could remember, she'd liked the old-fashioned ambience of the 1950s-style diner.

With its retro soda fountain, vintage jukebox and nostalgic memorabilia of Elvis and James Dean, the Starlight was pure Southern comfort.

Sam, who'd dined in upscale restaurants and artsy cafés worldwide, soaked in the relaxed atmosphere. Funny how the simple things here in Chestnut Grove had so much more meaning lately. But then, after Africa, everything had taken on more significance.

"Tham, Tham." Her nephew pounded chubby palms on the high chair's plastic tray. "Dink."

"Okay, buddy, coming right up."

She kissed the two-year-old's baby-scented hair, the familiar ache of loss and love filling her throat. She wanted so much for Gabriel that had been missing in her own life. In lieu of love, she'd had glamorous parties, constant travel and designer clothes, a lifestyle that bespoke success. But here was real success—in the bubbling laughter of a child.

Eric understood that. She was only beginning to, now that it was probably too late.

Sam waved the waitress over and ordered juice for the little one and coffee for herself. Sandra Lange, the diner's owner, noticed Gabriel and hurried over.

"Hello, little man," Sandra said. "I think you need a cookie." She looked to Sam for permission and when Sam nodded, Sandra produced a package of animal crackers from the pocket of a pink ruffled apron. Sam couldn't help noticing the pink breast-cancer bracelet sliding up and down the woman's right wrist, a reminder that other people had far more serious problems than she did.

"How are you doing, Sandra?" According to Sam's mother, the café owner had battled breast cancer a couple of years ago while searching for the child that had been taken from her at birth. That child had turned out to be Kelly Van Zandt. Just one more of the terrible heartaches Sam's grandfather had caused.

"Couldn't be better." With a fingernail, Sandra ripped open the package and handed an animal cracker to Gabriel.

"Cookie," he said and rewarded her with his toothy smile.

"I'm sorry for my family's part in all that's happened to you," Sam said.

"Honey, none of that has anything to do with you. You don't need to apologize." Sandra stepped aside when the waitress brought the drinks, then said, "I'm thankful the Lord allowed me to live long enough to have a relationship with my daughter. That's all that matters to me."

"I'm glad, too." And she meant it. Sometimes she was so ashamed of the Harcourt name. "Kelly's a terrific person."

Sandra patted her arm. "So are you, hon."

The statement took Sam aback. Could Sandra, with her world-wise eyes, see that Sam's totally together persona was nothing but a facade? And that on the inside she was a tangle of uncertainties, not even sure what she wanted out of life?

Unsettled, she busied herself by stirring the hot black coffee. Without sugar or cream the action was useless, but it gave her something to do with her hands.

"Can we get anything else for you, Sam?" Sandra asked.

"No, thank you. I'm meeting someone." As if waiting for his cue, the bell over the diner door jingled and Eric entered. The little tingle of awareness Sam experienced every time he appeared shimmied down her back.

"Good evening, Eric," Sandra said as he slid into the booth across from Sam. "Tea?"

Eric nodded. "Sweet and cold."

With her usual cheery smile, Sandra went off to fill the order.

"I see you brought company." Eric shook Gabriel's reaching hand and was rewarded with a glop of soggy cookie.

Mortified, Sam jumped up and grabbed for the napkins. "I am so sorry."

Eric laughed, teeth white and even in his dark face. "Not a problem. I worked in an orphanage, remember? I happen to like kids and their gooey messes."

Without thinking, Sam took his hand and carefully wiped the mess away. Instantly, she flashed to Africa, remembering the strength of that hand and how good his warm, calloused skin had felt against hers.

Samantha, the model, had schmoozed with princes and movie stars, but the touch of a missionary's hand had her blushing like a teenager. She released his fingers and sat back. When she looked up, Eric's expression was thoughtful as though he, too, remembered that time as special.

Thankful for the diversion Gabriel provided, Sam dug in the small diaper bag for Wet Wipes, using them to wash her nephew's hands and face. "My sister, Ashley, had a late class. I promised to babysit."

"That's what sisters are for, I guess."

"I'm glad to do it. Gabriel's an angel."

"He was an angel in the Bible, too."

"Really?"

"Yep. The angel who announced the birth of Christ."

"I didn't know that." Truthfully, she didn't know anything about the Bible, but Ashley had been talking about it a lot lately. Her sister was different, as were her parents since accepting the Lord. And after spending time with Eric and the kids from the youth group, Samantha was curious to know more.

Before she could ask, the waitress brought Eric's iced tea and refilled Sam's coffee cup.

Eric took a drink and let out a refreshed, masculine-sounding sigh of relief. "The heat out there today reminds me of Africa." The skin around his eyes crinkled. "Without the jackals, of course."

"I loved Africa," she said.

"Did you?" His dark eyes were serious above the tea glass.

"For the little time I was there, yes. It changed me. Made me think about things in a new way. I hope to go back someday."

"Me, too. Soon."

"For the boys?"

"And for the program. In order to get international adoptions going, I'll have to make frequent trips to meet the kids and the orphanage directors. I also got some great news from the Noble Foundation today."

Sam went very still, every nerve ending alert to his reaction. Now she understood why Eric was so upbeat tonight and hadn't even mentioned their disagreement over Gina. "What kind of news?"

As he explained the donation that had been made, Sam could sense his excitement. Rachel hadn't called to let her know, but from what Eric said, everything would go just as she had hoped. Most importantly, Eric would be in charge. He would do the right thing with the funds. She was certain of it.

"That's wonderful." Unsure how Eric would react if he discovered that she was the donor, Sam didn't want to pursue the topic too far. She was happy knowing that the wheels had been set into motion.

The salary she'd earned on the swimsuit shoot in Africa had gone into the fund. A ridiculous amount of money for cavorting on a beautiful, pristine beach. During her few hours at the orphanage, she'd made up her mind to donate the money, but after she'd returned to the States and landed the Style campaign, she could afford to be even more generous.

Gabriel, tired of being ignored by the adults, reached for Eric's tea. With uncanny reflexes, Eric caught the little hand, righted the tumbling glass and scooted sideways all in one quick movement. Tea and ice splashed out over the table.

Sam hopped up and began sopping the liquid with

paper napkins. "Eric, I am terribly sorry. Gabriel seems intent on getting your attention tonight."

Sandra noticed the commotion and brought a large sponge. When the mess was cleared away and Eric's glass replaced, Sam said, "Maybe we should discuss the picnic committee before Gabriel starts in on the rest of the café."

"Ah, the little guy is bored. Hey, Gabriel," he said to the baby and then took a clean napkin from the holder, using it to play a game of peekaboo. Gabriel's sweet, gurgling giggle had both adults laughing aloud.

"He's so adorable. I wish…" Sam caught herself. Wishes were useless. She already knew that. Nothing could change what the pursuit of perfection had done to her body, but remembering always cut like a dull blade. She fished in the diaper bag and came out with a toy to occupy her nephew, a set of colorful plastic keys to fit various slots in a ball.

Seeing the baby occupied, Eric wadded the napkin into a ball and tossed it on the table. "What's left to do for tomorrow?"

"The kids have everything ready. Nikki and I made a master list of all supplies, decorations, etcetera. This afternoon we borrowed a pickup truck to haul everything to the Noble Estate."

"Then the concession stand is already set up?" He lifted one of her manicured hands and teased. "Don't tell me you were on the business end of a hammer again?"

Warmth suffused Sam. She smiled into Eric's dancing eyes. He could be so charming most of the time. It felt good to be back on joking terms after he'd hurt her feelings over Gina. Maybe she had overreacted to the girl's upset stomach, but with her history, who wouldn't?

"Even though I am an experienced carpenter, as you well know." She wiggled her fingers beneath his. "The boys insisted on playing macho and finishing the job themselves."

"Too bad. A few bent nails would give the thing character."

"Careful, Pellegrino." She nodded toward Gabriel. "I have a secret weapon with me who could, at any moment, do something else unpleasant to you."

Eric eyed the baby with such mock terror that Sam laughed. "If you don't stop being silly we'll never get finished here."

"Worse things could happen."

Sam studied his expression. Was he saying he actually enjoyed her company again?

"Here's the duty schedule," she said, pulling a sheet from her purse. "Nikki and Gina worked this out and I haven't had time to check it over for accuracy."

"I can check it later. Did you make copies?"

"The girls did that, too. They've worked hard on this."

"I hope their hard work translates into a successful fund-raiser."

"Do you think the heat will keep people away?"

"You know this place better than I do, but I wouldn't think so. The estate is covered with big shade trees and there are plenty of drink stands."

"And don't forget the dunk tank," Sam said with a smile.

Eric laughed. "Yeah. People may be fighting to get dunked instead of the other way around."

Happiness bubbled up inside Samantha. She leaned back against the slick vinyl booth and pushed her hands up through the back of her hair, a gesture she used in modeling so often that it had become habit.

A young couple at a nearby table caught her eye. Staring at Samantha, the woman leaned forward and said something to the man, her expression animated. Hoping to avoid unwanted attention, Sam averted her face and sipped at her coffee.

Most of the time here in her hometown, she wasn't bothered, but not always. Chestnut Grove attracted a number of tourists, too, taking in the area history.

As the waitress dashed over to refill the cup, the pair got up and came toward Sam's booth. The woman carried something in one hand.

"Aren't you Samantha Harcourt? The model for Style jeans?"

So much for hoping they wouldn't say anything. With a polite, plastic smile, she answered, "Yes. I'm Sam."

"See, I told you it was her," the man said to his companion. "Go on. Ask her. She won't care."

The woman laid a magazine on the table. Sam's image filled the entire page. "Would you mind autographing this for me?"

The man whipped a pen from his pocket.

Eric grew quiet. Sam's heart sank to her pink French pedicure. Negative thoughts pushed into her head. Every time she and Eric found common ground, something happened to remind them both of the vast differences. He rescued orphans from lives of despair. She signed autographs for strangers. Boy, wasn't she special.

Chapter Six

This year's Noble Foundation Picnic, under the guidance of Andrew Noble, had morphed into the biggest fund-raiser ever. The expansive, manicured lawn of the Noble Estate was dotted with various types of games, concessions and other forms of entertainment. In the past the picnic had been an invitation-only affair. This year, the estate's massive electronic gates stood open to anyone willing to pay the price to enter the grounds.

A radio station broadcast from one side of the estate while a popular local television show, *Afternoons with Douglas Matthews,* filmed a segment near the green hedge maze. The Youth Center concession sat outside the maze opposite the film crew.

"They did it to us again, didn't they?"

With a wry shake of his head, Eric tacked the work schedule to a board inside the concession stand.

Nikki and Gina had scheduled him and Sam to work the stand together all day.

"Yes, and at least two of them will be jammed inside this booth throughout the day to keep an eye on us."

"And report back to the others." Though Eric doubted they'd have anything exciting to tell. His friendship with Samantha Harcourt was tentative at best.

Sam's perfect smile flashed, not the fake smile she'd used with the autograph seekers last night, but a smile that lit her from the inside out. She looked especially beautiful today in a lacy tank top and soft fitted jeans with just the right jewelry. Not that he was a fashion guru, but any man alive would notice Sam. Even casually dressed, she still looked like a glamorous model, a cut above every other woman in town.

As Rachel and Andrew had both intended, Samantha Harcourt would draw a crowd.

"Speaking of the connivers, here come Gina and Jeremy," she said.

Eric balanced a sleeve of paper cups onto the counter near the soft-drink machine and yelled, "Hi, guys. Where's the rest of the gang?"

"They'll be here," Jeremy said, ducking below the wooden frame to enter the booth. "Billy doesn't ever get out of bed before noon."

"That's why we put him on the second shift at the dunk tank." Gina followed her boyfriend inside. For once the girl wasn't wearing a sweater. In jeans and T-shirt, she was stick-thin, thinner even than Samantha.

Ever since Sam had shared her concern that Gina had an eating disorder, Eric had been watching. He hadn't admitted as much to Sam yet, but he, too, had begun to wonder if something was wrong. Gina was the perfect kid, a straight-A student, never any trouble to her parents and quiet as a mouse most of the time, but something didn't feel right.

Gina's gaze flicked to Sam and then away. Had Sam said something else to the girl? Later, when he and Sam were alone, he'd ask.

The thought brought him up short. Being alone with Sam sounded better than it should. Last night at the diner, they'd been having a great time until the couple had asked for her autograph. That reminder of the gulf between them had brought him down to earth. Samantha Harcourt, nearing supermodel status, was not in his league at all.

Now to convince the youth group of that.

"May I have a Coke, please?"

Eric turned his attention to their first customer. "One Coke coming up. Would you like some cotton candy, too? Fresh made by two of the *sweetest* teen-agers in town."

Gina and Jeremy groaned at his silly pun but quickly joined the fun of tempting customers to buy more than they'd come for. After all, this was a fund-raiser.

As the temperature climbed, the concession hopped with thirsty customers. People swarmed the grounds of the plantation. The wholesome, relaxed atmosphere brought out families and children to enjoy the myriad activities for a good cause. Hamburgers and barbecue scented the air. Laughter drifted through the enormous trees. Rachel's concerns about the heat proved unwarranted.

Eric was squirting mustard on a hot dog when he heard a customer say, "Miss Harcourt, would you mind taking a picture with me?"

Sam, busy scooping ice into cups, stiffened. If he hadn't been standing next to her, her sweet perfume mesmerizing him, Eric would never have been aware of her reaction. Her million-dollar smile beamed at the admirer.

"I'd love to have a picture with you." She dried her hands. "But this is a fund-raising event, you know. Everything has a price."

Eric bit back a bark of surprised laughter. Now, that was one smart lady.

For a second, the fan was taken aback but then she handed her camera to her husband. "What a great idea."

"In fact, why don't we get both of you in this? Eric can snap the photo." Sam ducked outside the booth and stood between the couple while Eric pressed the shutter and collected the money. Sam promised to autograph the developed photo.

When the couple left, someone else appeared. "Are you taking pictures with your fans?"

"For a price." Mischief danced in Sam's eyes.

Within moments, the grounds were buzzing with word that Samantha Harcourt was taking photos with anyone willing to pay the fee. A line formed outside the concession.

"You've created a monster," Eric said as he fielded

cameras while Sam posed and the kids hawked sodas and hot dogs.

Ben and Leah Cavanaugh strolled by, pushing baby Joseph in a stroller. When their daughter, Olivia, saw what was happening, she insisted on a photo, too. Sam knelt beside the little girl and hugged her. Olivia, lively and bright, was thrilled.

"Wait till I tell Daniel," she squealed, mentioning Andrew and Miranda Jones's young son. "He'll be so jealous."

Sam patted Olivia's back. "Tell him to come on over and have a picture with us."

"You and me both?"

"Sure. Why not?" She beamed a smile at the Cavanaughs. "What do you say, Mom and Dad?"

Ben laughed. "I think you're a master at raising money."

"Good. The kids are worth it."

As Eric watched Sam work her charm on the gathering, his admiration notched upward. From her initial reaction, she didn't particularly enjoy this, but she was generous enough to use her celebrity for something worthwhile.

Generous, smart, kind, hardworking. Adjectives he'd never expected to use with Sam. His conscience poked at him. He'd thought all those things about her in Africa, so what had happened? Was his ego so fragile that he was still smarting about the identity mix-up? Or had his bad attitude toward the rich caused him to misjudge her?

In his younger days, he'd sometimes been jealous

of the wealthy. Growing up in a large family that pinched pennies had marked him, and getting dumped by a socialite in college hadn't helped. But he thought he'd outgrown the poor-boy chip on his shoulder. Maybe not.

He rubbed at his chest, aware of the hollowness there, a sure sign he and the Lord needed to have a conversation.

A burst of laughter brought his attention back to the moment. Gina and Samantha were bent double, laughing at Jeremy who preened and posed in imitation of Sam. The long line of customers had dwindled away, at least for the time being.

"Oh, Miss Harcourt," Jeremy said in a falsetto voice. "May I please have that paper cup you drank from? I'll cherish it forever."

Gina and Sam giggled again, but Eric detected a note of embarrassment in Sam's laughter.

"Hey," he said, gesturing to Gina and Jeremy. "You two get over here and let Sam take your picture for a change."

"Do you have a camera?"

"Sure. Got my digital. We need pictures for the church newsletter anyway."

Jeremy hopped out of the concession stand and flexed a bicep. "Gotta love this, huh, Gina?"

Gina rolled her eyes. "Don't encourage him, Eric. He's already conceited enough."

But, using an ancient oak trunk as background, the young couple mugged for the camera. Sam took several shots and then waved to Eric.

"Get over there with them."

Joining the fun, he let her take his picture, first with Gina and then with Jeremy, both males behaving in typical macho manner.

A customer arrived and Gina scuttled back into the stand to take care of business. Sam turned, ready to join her, when Eric caught a lock of her pale hair and gave a gentle tug. She looked over her shoulder, silvery eyes questioning, perfect lips curved upward.

As if he'd jumped out of an airplane, Eric's belly dipped.

"Don't I get a picture with the famous lady?"

Face alight with humor, she wheeled around and stuck out a palm. "What's it worth to ya, big boy?"

A lot more than he wanted to admit.

"A big spender like me? Let's see…" Keeping it light, he reached into his pocket and pulled out a twenty. "How's this?"

With finger and thumb, she snapped the bill from his hand. "Since it's your camera, I guess a mere twenty will do."

Eric handed the camera to Jeremy. "Take the picture, Jer, before the price goes up. Inflation, you know."

Still playing around, Eric looped an arm across Sam's shoulders to strike a pose. Her spicy scent enveloped him. He went light-headed, all the silliness draining away. The women at work wore perfumes that smelled great. Why did Sam's have this effect on him?

To his pleasure and discomfort, Sam slid an arm around his waist and tilted her head onto his shoulder.

The action was innocent and intentionally flirty, just a pose for the camera. This was something Samantha did all the time, and yet Eric's pulse kicked up a notch.

Catapulted back in time, Eric recalled a hot, starry night in Africa when, for a brief space in time, he'd imagined Sam to be the woman he'd been praying for.

His head whirled with a startling question: What would it feel like to hold Sam in his arms for real? To follow the dream that had begun on a faraway continent?

Sam didn't want to move. She longed to stand right here under the old shade tree with Eric's side pressed to hers and her head on his strong, muscled shoulder. He smelled wonderful, like laundry soap and cotton candy with a tantalizing dollop of something entirely Eric.

What had begun as a joke had taken on new meaning.

The camera flashed, and Eric stepped away. Sam felt the loss bone deep.

When Eric seemed unaffected, Sam decided she was full of nonsense today. Taking care of Gabriel had made her feel domestic, needy, as though her biological clock were ticking.

Yeah, right. Her biological clock.

She shook away the bitter regret. A busy mind had no time to dwell on what could never be. With a vengeance, she began reorganizing the wares inside the booth.

"Is it okay if Jeremy and I go check out the rest of the picnic now?" Gina asked.

"Go ahead. You've earned a break," Eric said. "Just remember to come back and tell us if we're missing anything great."

"Take a hot dog with you." Sam quickly slapped together two dogs and pushed them toward the teens. "You've worked hard. You must be starved by now."

"Hey, cool." Jeremy took both hot dogs in one long hand. "Thanks, Sam."

As the kids walked away, Jeremy offered one to Gina, who shook her head.

The warning bells in Sam's mind grew louder. Though she'd tried talking to Gina again, the result had been exactly zero. She'd considered calling the teen's parents but they only knew Sam as a member of the notorious Harcourt family. And if she was wrong, everyone, including Eric, would be upset with her.

But a nagging voice inside asked, *What if you're right?*

"You're still worried about Gina, aren't you?" Eric asked softly.

She turned to find him watching her, brown eyes thoughtful.

"Very. I know there's a problem, even if you don't believe me."

"Maybe I do."

She blinked, surprised. "But you said—"

"I know what I said, but you're not the hysterical type. You must have a legitimate reason for your suspicions."

She wondered when he'd decided that, but didn't ask. Hearing the admission was enough—for now.

"I've seen this kind of thing too many times in the modeling industry. Gina's in trouble."

"What can we do?"

"I don't know at this point. She needs professional help, at least counseling and maybe even a treatment facility. I wish I knew her family."

"I know them. The Sharpes are good people."

"Would you consider talking to them about the situation?"

He backed against the counter and crossed his arms, eyebrows dipped in thought. "You know more about this stuff than I do. I wouldn't know what to say."

Sam sighed and stared up into the rustling leaves of the giant oak. A squirrel stared back and she couldn't even muster a smile. Gina was killing herself and Sam was helpless to stop her.

"Hey, don't look so glum." Eric gave her elbow a gentle shake. "I didn't say I wouldn't talk to the Sharpes. But I'd need help. Would you be there with me?"

A weight lifted off Sam's shoulders.

"I'll do anything to keep another girl from going through what I—" She stopped, bit down on her bottom lip, afraid she'd said too much.

She had. Eric was far too smart and intuitive to miss the clues.

His dark chocolate eyes searched her face, as understanding dawned. "You've been there, haven't you? You're coming at this from personal experience."

The lively noise of the picnic faded away as Sam considered how to answer. Across the way, a clown sold colorful helium balloons to a little girl with red ribbons in her hair. One of the balloons escaped and rose high into the sky. Sam looked up, following its ascent.

Like the balloon, she could escape with a lot of hot air or she could trust a man who had dedicated his life to helping people. She'd carried the burden alone for a long time, and she was tired. But she was also ashamed and embarrassed. Eric's opinion of her was important, although she wasn't sure why. Only in recent days had he begun to be less prickly in her company. Would he think less of her if he knew the whole truth?

"Sam?" he questioned gently. "That's why you're so worried about Gina, isn't it?"

She brought her gaze back to his and locked on. He was a missionary, or had been. He must care about people all the way down to his soul. Behind the laughter and wit was a steadfastness, a strength that encouraged confidence. But could she trust Eric Pellegrino with her ugly secret?

Swallowing past a lump of anxiety, she gripped the rough wooden counter with both hands and murmured, "I've never told anyone except my doctors."

Eric pushed away from the counter and moved closer, as though his nearness could erase her pain and humiliation. She wanted him to hold her, which was crazy. Instead, he touched her shoulder, but the simple gesture of human contact brought inexplicable comfort.

"You can tell me."

And so, over the next few minutes, she shared the distorted thinking that had led to an eating disorder, and the demanding career that had kept her trapped for so many years. She told of the hospital stay and the treatment facility, of the ongoing struggle with negative voices inside her head.

By the time she stopped, he was leaning against the counter, ankles crossed, listening intently. His quiet acceptance bolstered her, making the story easier to tell.

"Have you ever wondered why?" he asked.

She hitched a shoulder. Of course she had. Deep inside, she was empty, always striving for a perfection she could not attain, a need to be more than she was. But she didn't tell him that.

"The therapists have theories. They've blamed my unemotional upbringing, my perfectionist tendencies, the need for control. And of course, the pressure of staying ultra-thin in a highly competitive profession. All I know is that food becomes an anorexic's greatest passion and her deepest fear. We have trouble thinking about anything else." She gave a self-conscious shake of her head and stared toward the TV program in progress across the way. "I don't know why I told you this. You must think I'm a total loser."

"I think you're amazing."

She spun toward him, shocked. "Me? Amazing because I can figure fat content and count calories in my head?"

The corners of his eyes crinkled. "Because you haven't let a serious illness stop you. Because you're trying to find a way to help Gina so she doesn't have to go through what you have. You're a fighter, Sam. I admire fighters."

"Sorry, I don't see it. I wish I agreed with you, but I know better. I still have to journal what I eat every single day so I don't regress. And the negative thoughts never stop. Never."

"Quit beating yourself up. Look at the good you're trying to do."

She made a face. "And failing. Gina won't listen at all."

Eric laid a finger next to his mouth and then pointed at her. "I've got an idea. Why don't you come to my Sunday school class and talk about eating disorders? You don't have to share your personal story, just talk in general about the modeling industry and the pressure to be thin. Tell about the other girls you've known who have eating disorders. Gina may not be the only girl battling this."

"I can almost promise you she's not."

Sam bent to pick up a discarded paper cup, thinking about the offer. If someone had talked to her in high school, she might have gotten help sooner. She might even be a whole woman today.

She tossed the cup into a trash bag and dusted her hands. "Do you think they'll listen?"

"Are you kidding? Haven't you noticed how Tiffany's been wearing her hair like yours? They admire you, Sam. They'll listen because of who you are and the success you've had."

The more she thought about it, the more the idea appealed. Maybe she could do this. Maybe she could stop the madness in some other girl's life. Eric wasn't inclined to flattery. If he thought she could make a difference, she could.

Excitement began to simmer in her veins. "I'll do it."

"Awesome." Eric slapped her hand in a high five. He looked as excited by the prospect as she felt. "After you speak, I'll follow up with an applicable lesson from the Bible. Together we'll be a winning team."

"The Bible talks about anorexia?"

"Not specifically, but God does talk about our bodies and how we're to treat them. Psalms says we are fearfully and wonderfully made. Get that, Sam? When God made you, you were already wonderful. He knew you before you were even born and loved you just the way you are."

For someone who had trouble loving herself most of the time, the idea of a loving God didn't seem feasible. "I've never given God much thought."

"Maybe you should. He's pretty awesome." Eric turned toward the soda fountain and filled two cups. "Here. Drink. It's hot out here."

"I'm okay."

Eric lasered her with a firm look. "Drink it, Miss Harcourt. It's lemonade. Vitamin C and all that."

"Pushy, aren't you?" But she sipped the cold

drink anyway. "Can I ask you something? About God, I mean?"

"Absolutely. I have Sociology and divinity degrees. Let me wow you with my deep, insightful knowledge."

Sam laughed. "Well, Mr. Deep and Insightful, tell me what's so great about being a Christian. I mean, how is your life different from any other? Did all your problems suddenly disappear when you accepted Christ?"

Eric made a disparaging noise in the back of his throat. "You were in Africa. You already know better than that. Problems don't go away. The Lord just helps us deal with them. And the Bible is our rule book so we know the right way to handle whatever comes along." He sipped his drink. When she didn't say anything, he looked adorably sheepish and asked, "Was that too preachy?"

"Not at all. I was thinking about what you said. My family has changed so much since they became believers. They've tried to explain how they feel but I don't get it."

"Come to church with me. Give God a try. He won't let you down."

"What if I let Him down?" She could hardly believe they were having this conversation. A week ago, Eric had treated her like a pariah, but something had changed today.

"He'll forgive you. I know that from personal experience. Christians aren't perfect. We're just saved, with a ticket to heaven, bought with a price."

"Bought with a price? I don't know what you mean by that."

"The price was God's son. You were worth God's only son. Which makes you a real special lady, Samantha Harcourt."

She'd been called *special* before in modeling circles, but from Eric the words weren't flattery. They were real.

Could Eric and her family be right? The whole God thing seemed to be working for them. Could a relationship with God be the missing ingredient in her own life? At this point in her restless, dissatisfied existence, Samantha was willing to check out every option.

At that moment, Kelly and Ross Van Zandt came up, and Sam turned her attention to them. As Eric fixed their hot dogs, he told them about Sam's fundraising efforts, calling the idea brilliant. Basking in his praise and their congratulations, she filled the soft drinks.

After a minute of chitchat, the couple ambled away, and Sam's attention was drawn to Kelly's gently rounded belly. She touched her own very flat one. What would it be like to carry a child beneath her heart? A child that was half her and half the man she loved?

Her gaze flickered to Eric, but she caught the thought and tossed it away.

In between filling soft-drink orders for a smattering of customers and a few more requests for photos, she and Eric talked some more. Talked the way Sam had longed to do since meeting Eric again.

He was witty and kind and surprisingly wise for

such a young guy. Chocolate-brown eyes and a handsome face didn't hurt, either. The attraction she'd felt for him in Africa was back with a vengeance. And Sam wasn't sure if that was a good thing or a bad thing.

Chapter Seven

Eric counted out change for a ten dollar bill, pleased to see the cash box stuffed with money from their efforts so far. They could order school supplies for a lot of needy African kids after today.

Sam, dangly earrings glinting in the sunlight, smiled for another photograph with two teenage girls. Her laughter drifted over him as sweet as her perfume.

Today's picnic had changed everything. Sam wasn't some snobbish celebrity taking pity on the peons as he'd thought. She was real. A woman with hurts and sorrows like everyone else. She was just better at hiding them than most. A woman Eric had totally misread.

"Lord, forgive me," he mumbled. He'd been a jerk, a judgmental fool who'd looked on the outside instead of getting to know Sam as a person.

And now that he'd awakened to that truth, he wanted to know her better. As stunned and saddened as he'd been by her anorexia story, he'd been deeply impressed, too. She was strong, whether she knew it or not, a woman doing the best she could.

He didn't know a lot about eating disorders but he planned to research, and if he could help Sam in any way, he'd do it. She needed God's help a lot more than his, though, and he'd pray that she would come to understand how much the Lord cared about her. At least she had promised to come to church and talk to his Sunday school class. That was a start for both Sam and the kids.

"Penny for your thoughts," Sam said as she slid back into the booth.

"I was thinking about you," he admitted and was rewarded by the spark of interest in her face.

"Oh, yeah?"

"Yeah." He left it there, knowing she heard compliments all the time. Anything he said would sound like flattery.

She nodded toward the left side of the rambling green maze. "Isn't that Douglas Matthews coming this way?"

"They must be finished filming the show."

"Rumor says the networks are after him to go syndicated. That would be a big feather for Chestnut Grove."

"I heard that, but I'm not much on talk shows. Too busy," Eric said. And tall, good-looking guys didn't do a thing for him. The women, however, seemed to go crazy for Doug's blue eyes and genial charm.

"It's a good show, mainly because of Douglas's

personality. He really knows how to work an audience and get the best out of his guests."

"Do you know him?"

"Not at all."

"Looks like you're about to be introduced."

The talk show host, impeccably dressed and looking cool even in the August heat, approached the concession stand.

"Hello, Samantha, I'm Douglas Matthews." He extended a hand; a diamond ring winked in the sunlight. "Doug, of course." His smile was as bright and perfect as Sam's.

Sam shook his hand before turning to Eric. "This is Eric Pellegrino. He's the assistant director at Tiny Blessings Adoption Agency."

Doug's smile faltered a little bit. "A pleasure, Eric."

He gave a quick nod in Eric's direction and then returned his charm to Samantha.

"Would you like a soda or something?" Sam asked politely.

"Actually, I stopped by to ask you a question. I'll get right to the point. I'd like you to be on my show."

Sam blinked twice. "Me? Why?"

The talk-show host laughed, his pearly whites stunning. His fingers found Sam's again and squeezed. Eric felt an inappropriate surge of jealousy.

"You're Samantha Harcourt, the biggest thing to come out of Chestnut Grove. Your fans would love to see you on my show. You can talk about your career, the famous people you've worked with, where you're going next, anything you like. We can even do a segment on your beautiful home. Fans love to hear the inside scoop on how the stars live. Come on, what do you say?"

Eric, who felt about as necessary to this conversation as a raincoat in the desert, watched Sam for her reaction. Would she jump at the offer of more attention, of more opportunity for the world to admire her?

Interestingly enough, Sam didn't answer right away. As if the decision was far harder than the one she'd made a few minutes ago, she gnawed prettily at her lower lip.

Eric had a hard time not staring. Sam had a beautiful mouth, one he'd almost kissed once upon a time.

He shook his head, dispelling the crazy thoughts.

"I'm sorry, Doug. I'll have to say no this time. I'm on hiatus right now, and the last thing I want is more publicity with everything that's going on in my family."

Doug's golden smile faded. The blue eyes that had sparkled with friendliness narrowed. "Oh, come on. I'd consider it a personal favor. I'll call your agent, if you insist, though being a hometown girl and all…" He leaned forward, as if sharing a secret. "Look, Sam, this really *would* be a personal favor. The National networks are looking at my show. Having you on would be a coup."

She shook her head. "I'm sorry."

He straightened and whipped out a business card. "Don't say no. Say maybe. Talk to your agent if you must. Have him give me a call."

With an air of confidence that grated on Eric's nerves, Matthews lifted Sam's hand, turned it over, laid the card in her palm and closed her fingers over it one by one. "Better yet, *you* give me a call."

With a wink, he strutted off toward the maze.

Eric ground his back teeth together. Although Eric was pretty sure the guy was married, Douglas behaved like a Casanova. Before he could think better of it, Eric imitated the talk-show host in a silly voice. "Give me a call, Sam. You know you want me."

Sam burst out laughing and thumped his shoulder. "You're a nut. A nice nut, but still a little goofy."

"Are you going on his show?"

"I don't know. Probably not. I would feel stupid appearing on TV in my own hometown to talk about myself. Kind of pretentious, don't you think?"

Boy, had he ever misjudged this woman. "And here I was thinking you'd love the attention."

"Sometimes I do," she admitted. "But right now, I'm not sure what I want. The people in this town have known me since I was a baby and yet they treat me differently because of my career. I'm still just plain Samantha Harcourt who wore braces in junior high and got a D in American History."

Eric stifled a laugh. She would never be "just plain" anything. "How could you get a D in American History when you live this close to so much of it? Jamestown, Williamsburg, Yorktown. Virginia's the birthplace of America."

She rolled her glorious eyes. "You sound like my

history teacher. Today, history is interesting. Back then, it was—" she stuck a finger into her check and twisted "—bo-ring."

They were both still chuckling when Nikki and Billy approached the stand. Nikki, black kohl eyeliner melting in the heat, looked like a raccoon. Eric thought he'd probably better not tell her that.

"Someone over at the dunk tank wants Eric to come take a turn," Nikki said.

"Me? In the tank?" One of the kids, he figured, but which one?

Nikki's lips kicked up in an ornery grin. "Yes, sir. We'll take over here if you'll go there."

"What can I say?" He leaped over the board frame onto the soft grass. "Anything for a good cause."

He had already started in that direction when he heard Sam call, "Hold up there, mister. I'm coming, too."

When she was at his side, he said, "You couldn't resist seeing me dunked, could you?"

"Nope."

She hummed a little tune and behaved in such a suspicious manner, he asked, "What are you up to?"

By now they were at the dunk tank. She stuck her hands in her back pockets and rocked back on her heels, laughing.

"I'm the one paying to see you dunked."

Sam watched Eric climb into the dunk tank and take his place on the swing. She'd been a little nervous when she, Gina and Jeremy had cooked up the scheme, but Eric hadn't disappointed them. Good sport that he was, he challenged them all to come and get him.

Sam took a turn first, aiming the ball at a metal paddle that would release the swing and send Eric plunging into a pool of cold water. The first throw missed by a mile.

"Come on, Sam. You throw like a girl," Eric taunted.

"Get him, Sam," someone behind her called. A glance back told her they were drawing a crowd. Good. More money for kids.

She wound up and tried again, coming woefully short. The catcalls from Eric increased. "I knew you couldn't do it. Sissy girl."

"I still have one more throw." With fierce determination, she blocked out his voice and aimed at the lever.

"You can't hit me. You can't hit me," Eric taunted just as she released the ball.

Clang! The lever released. Startled, Eric threw his hands into the air and plunged into the pool.

He came up sputtering. Sam didn't know who laughed more, her or Eric. Making all kinds of nonsensical threats, he climbed back onto the seat, ready to go again.

Sam accepted the back slaps and congratulations of the teenagers and a growing group of onlookers. She stepped aside to let the next person have a turn while she took over the ticket sales.

After about an hour, the line thinned out. "Dunking me is getting boring," Eric said as he stepped out of the tank and reached for a towel. "We need a new victim to recharge the crowd." He shot Sam a knowing look.

"Uh-uh," she said. "Not me."

He grabbed her arm, holding on while he shook his head like a shaggy dog and sprinkled her with water. "Why not? Afraid you'll melt?"

Sam squealed. The cold water was startling in this August heat.

"Come on, Sam," Jeremy urged. "Think of those little kids in Africa. If anyone can draw a crowd, it's you." He jerked a pair of eyebrows at her. "What's the matter? You chicken?"

"Me? Chicken? Not on your life, buddy boy." She poked at him with one finger, then slipped off her sandals, handed her bracelets to Gina and headed toward the enclosure.

Eric, drying his hair with a towel, looked up, eyes wide with surprise. "Are you serious?"

"As a heart attack." And then before she could change her mind, she hopped onto the seat and thought about the kids in Africa.

Later that evening, when the picnic ended and the cleanup crew swarmed the grounds, Eric's body ached but his spirit was full. The long, exhausting day had been even more successful than he'd imagined. He glanced at his cochair. Somehow, Sam still looked beautiful, though she had to be as weary as anyone. When he'd helped her out of the dunk tank and draped a towel around her shoulders, he'd been close enough to see the fatigue behind the laughter.

He still couldn't believe she'd done it. Not only had she worked in the tank longer than anyone, she'd figured a way to wrangle more money out of the customers. He had to admit he was impressed. The beautiful model who was paid to look good hadn't been a bit fazed as she took plunge after plunge into the cold pool and came up drenched.

"Today was fun." He clinked the lid closed on the stuffed cash box in preparation for turning the proceeds in to Andrew's staff inside the house. "Exhausting but fun."

"It was, wasn't it?" Her hair had dried by now and hung straight and flat against her head. She fluffed it with her fingertips. "I must look hideous."

"You look gorgeous," he said easily.

Cash box swinging between them, they fell in step toward the house. Security lights had taken the place of the sun, and the trees cast shadows across the lawn. The cleanup crews would need several days to put the plantation back to its usual manicured perfection.

"Sorry," she said. "I wasn't fishing for a compliment."

"You got one anyway. You'd look good no matter what." He grinned and flexed his shoulders. "Like me. We just can't help ourselves."

She laughed and shook her head. "When we first started this project, I thought the two of us would never laugh together. But we've done plenty of that today."

They deposited the cash box and signed out with the other volunteers before heading toward the parking area. The teenagers had long since abandoned ship. Other volunteers still milled the grounds or the parking lot, but most were also gone.

"When we started this project, I was a jerk," Eric admitted. "I owe you an apology." She didn't press him for details and he was glad. "Forgive me?"

"I'm just glad we're friends again."

Yeah, friends. He could do that. He could be friends with Samantha until she went back to Chicago and her own kind of people.

When they reached her car, he opened the door for her. She didn't get in. Instead, she stood in the opening, facing him.

Eric rested a forearm on the top edge of the car door. "I could pick you up tomorrow for church," he said. "Afterwards, we could have lunch."

Sam smoothed the hair back from her forehead. "I'd like that."

She didn't get inside her sports car and Eric was glad. He was equally reluctant to end their day. Not since Africa had he felt this content or had this much fun.

That night outside the orphanage, he'd almost kissed her, but he hadn't known then that hers was one of the best known faces in the country. He was probably crazy for even thinking such a thing, but he wanted to kiss her now even more. Not because she was Samantha Harcourt, the successful model, but because she was Sam, the awesome woman.

He moved in, felt the warmth of her breath against his cheek, saw her lips part the tiniest bit.

Then someone called his name.

Chapter Eight

A week later the memory of that near-kiss still lingered in Eric's mind. He'd wanted to be irked at Scott Crosby for the interruption, but the new assistant pastor couldn't help it if his tire was flat and he didn't have a jack. So, like a Good Samaritan, Eric had waved goodbye to Sam when he'd really wanted to kiss her, and then gone to help Scott with his car.

Unfortunately, the moment was lost and in the week since the picnic no other opportunity had come his way. He was pretty disappointed about that, though he knew better than to get too involved with a woman of Sam's caliber. Even though he now knew her to be a terrific person, she was still far out of his league. He didn't even know where she stood on the crucial issue of adoption.

Yet, Gina's problem had thrown them together once again, and this morning he was glad to have Sam by his side at church.

He glanced at her, sitting in the corner of his Sunday school classroom, hands gripped tightly in her lap. He'd known she was nervous as she'd spoken with his students, but the teenagers hadn't appeared to notice. Some of the kids hadn't met her before and they'd been awed to have a success- ful model as their key speaker. Even now, after he'd taken over, the class was quieter and listen- ing with more intensity than usual. Sam's talk about eating disorders and peer pressure had gotten to them.

"Being a teenager today is tough," he said to the rows of faces. "Other than the pressure for girls to be thin and guys to be buff, where do you personally feel pressured?"

"Making good grades," someone said.

"Being cool. In the right crowd at school," said another. "Sometimes other kids think I'm a dweeb because I don't party."

"Yeah, but they respect you, too," Nikki said. "You can be cool and be a Christian."

The other kids chuckled. Individualist Nikki demanded respect from everyone. He doubted any- one had dared criticize the black stripe running down the center her hair.

"Good point." Eric looked around at the group of sixteen teens, each one as different as Africa from Virginia. "Any others?"

"Drinking."

"Excellent. Others. Come on, what's the biggie?"

"Sex?" one of the girls murmured and then

glanced down at her Bible, face flushing bright red. The rest of the class tittered.

"Yeah. Big-time." Eric nodded. In a mixed group, he didn't want to go too deep into the subject but the kids needed to hear God's directive in every area of their lives. "And yet, if you give in, your self-esteem tumbles lower. The cool news is this—you don't have to handle any issue alone. God says to trust and rely on him, not on yourself. Letting anything control you or pressure you for long is not only counterproductive, it's sin. Even God isn't trying to control you. He wants what's best for you. He loves who you are, the way you are."

"Okay," one of the girls said, "but you feel pretty worthless when you're the only fat kid in class or you don't make the basketball team. It's hard to remember that God thinks you're okay the way you are."

"I know that, guys." Eric stepped from behind his teaching podium, his thoughts drifting to Sam, though he trained his gaze on the teens. "Even adults face times when their self-worth plummets. Remember that when you feel worthless like Sam said, God doesn't feel that way about you. Think about it. He loved you enough to send his only son to die in your place. You are worth everything to God. When the worthless thoughts come, replace them with that thought. You were worth God's son. Read the Bible. Find out what God has to say about you. You'll be surprised to discover just how truly special you are. Then when you're feeling down or stressed out, when something comes along that you can't handle, meditate on the things you've learned. God's word is truth. Anything contradictory is a lie. God will give you the tools to not only face life's challenges, but to feel good about who you are and what your purpose in life is all about."

He felt Sam staring at him, soaking in every word. He'd planned this message as much for her as for the kids because she needed to understand how special she was in God's eyes.

He glanced at his watch. "We have about a minute. Anybody have a question or a last quick comment?"

"Can we talk about this again next week?" Tiffany asked. "Especially about the whole self-esteem, body-image thing? And how God is supposed to help us deal with that stuff?"

"Sure. I'll bring in more scripture references, and we'll dig into the Bible and find out exactly what God has to say about it." He looked at Sam. "Can you be here?"

Every teenage head swiveled in her direction. Sam nodded and stood, pulling a handful of business cards from a fancy-looking purse, her wide-belted skirt swishing around her knees.

"If any of you need to talk, if you have a problem, especially about your weight or fitness, call me. I brought cards with my cell number. Please don't share them with the world. They're only for you. But if I can help, give me a call."

As the kids crowded around Samantha, Eric smiled to himself. Good thing he didn't have an enormous ego. Otherwise, he'd feel like a leftover sandwich. The kids had all but ignored him in their quest for one of Sam's personal cards.

The dismissal bell chimed and in a rush of scraping chairs and noisy kids, the room emptied.

"You were great. Absolutely terrific," he told Sam.

"So were you."

Eric offered his elbow and was gratified when Sam slid her hand into the crook. "We're a good team. I think you may get some phone calls."

She gnawed at that full lower lip, a habit he'd noted when she was concerned about something. "I hope Gina will be one of them."

"Maybe things will work out with her parents."

"I hope so. I took her to lunch last week with Nikki and another of their friends. Gina ordered a salad, no dressing and a cup of black coffee. Coffee was one of my fillers. It gives you energy that you don't really have, a false sense of being functional. If she gets any thinner, she's going to do some serious damage to herself."

"If she hasn't already."

"Exactly," Sam said grimly.

He'd asked the Sharpes, Gina's parents, for a short meeting today after church. He prayed they would be receptive.

Sam's hand still tucked into his elbow, he led the way into the sanctuary. Eric couldn't believe how good and right that simple action felt.

A few friends glanced their way, smiled and nodded. Anne Williams elbowed her husband, Caleb, who turned in his pew and grinned at them.

Eric resisted the temptation to scowl back.

He and Sam were friends. They'd grown to like each other. Maybe a lot. But she was an extremely successful model, and he was a lowly missionary turned adoption specialist trying to adopt two African boys. Sam was so far out of his league, it wasn't even funny.

Not funny at all.

Sam settled into the pew beside Eric, surprisingly comfortable in the beautiful old church. Three rows up, she spotted her parents and sister with little Gabriel. Her nephew spotted her, too, and grinned, a simple act that felt like a long-distance hug. Loving her sister's baby had become the most meaningful thing in her life.

She scanned around to catch sight of Gina, finally noticing her sandwiched in between Jeremy and Nikki to the far right. The girl had been extremely quiet during Sunday school this morning, and Sam was afraid for her. Nothing she or Eric said seemed to penetrate the wall of denial Gina had built around her illness. Their last best hope was Gina's parents. Surely, they could see how thin and pale their daughter had become. Even her dark brown hair was dull and lifeless.

Eric reached for a hymnal and opened to a page apparently announced while she'd been wool gathering. The movement stirred his morning shower-and-shave lotion, though Sam tried not to notice. This was church, after all, and she felt ashamed to be thinking how good Eric looked and smelled. But they were, by nature of the crowded church, squeezed in close to one another. And Sam wasn't a bit sorry about that.

The music began, filling the sanctuary with a joyful noise. She felt good about this morning's talk in Sunday school. Maybe she'd needed to speak about her experience as much as Gina had needed to hear it. As nervous as she'd been beforehand, she was glad Eric had talked her into speaking.

His arm brushed hers and she tried to focus on the words of the song. But again her mind strayed to something Eric had said. He claimed God loved people exactly the way they were. She had a hard time understanding what that meant. Did God love the perfectionism that drove her? Did He love the mess she'd made of her life? Or did He love her in spite of those things? From her experience, looking perfect was the only reason people cared about her. Would God be any different?

Eric said He was. Since the picnic she and the former missionary had talked by phone and had lunch a couple of times. She'd felt like the Serengeti during the rainy season as she'd soaked in his friendship and Godly counsel. They'd talked in depth about eating disorders in preparation for church today, and Eric's Christian perspective was helping change the way she thought about everything.

Even her negative thoughts had grown quieter this week. They weren't gone, but they hadn't been a constant source of torment, either.

According to Eric, forgiveness was possible for everyone. But Sam hadn't asked if forgiveness extended to someone who'd stupidly and intentionally damaged her own body. The questions played over and over inside her head as the music ended and Reverend Fraser began the sermon.

The title of the message grabbed her attention: God Uses Broken Vessels. Then the minister went on to tell story after story of people in the Bible who were terribly weak, sometimes sinful, and yet God forgave them and used them to do amazing things. Abraham lied to protect his own skin. King David murdered to hide his adultery. On and on the stories went while Sam listened in growing amazement. She'd thought the Bible characters were all perfect holy people. That Christians must be perfect, too, or lose God's love. But according to the pastor and today's scriptures, neither appeared to be true.

Like a delicate rose, hope budded.

She'd tried a lot of things in her pursuit of happiness and perfection. None of them had satisfied for long. Would religion be any different?

The answer came on swift wings as she noted the glow on her sister's young face, a joy that was repeated on many of the worshippers. Many of them had something she didn't. Something she wanted.

The minister closed the sermon and asked if anyone needed prayer.

Sam could hardly contain her nervous anticipation. She wanted prayer, but she wanted it from someone she knew and trusted.

Fingers trembling, her mouth dry, she touched Eric's arm. He leaned sideways so she could whisper in his ear. "I want Christ in my life. What do I do?"

The smile on Eric's face would stay with her forever. As if they were the only two people in the church, he turned to face her, took her hand in both of his and gazed deeply into her eyes.

And then he led her through a simple prayer to Jesus.

Eric could hardly contain the thrill running through his veins. Leading someone to the Lord was always exciting, but this was Sam. Her fingers trembled in his, and when the prayer ended, tears slipped over her perfect cheekbones. Eric understood completely.

"Thank you," she whispered, smile tremulous.

"No thanks needed. It was a privilege." He wanted to say more, to encourage her and give her time to debrief what had just occurred, but the pastor dismissed the service and people began to move around. He didn't want to embarrass her, but he was so thrilled he wanted to take the minister's microphone and share the news. He wouldn't, though. It was hers to share.

Her sister, Ashley, came toward them, her little boy at her side. When he spotted his aunt Sam, the toddler pumped his short legs up and down in an excited stationary jig. Giving a mighty tug on his mother's hand, he pulled loose and rushed through the crowd.

"Tham, Tham."

Sam scooped him up for a big hug. "Hi, Gabriel."

"I think he likes you," Eric said.

"You think?" Sam's face, already glowing, beamed.

Her nephew noticed the residual tears and patted at her cheeks, expression puzzled and concerned. About that time, Ashley arrived to claim her son.

"I have news, Ash," Sam said as she handed the child to his mother. "I accepted the Lord today."

Ashley looked from Sam to Eric and back again. "No kidding?" And then, baby and all, she grabbed her sister in a big hug. "I'm so glad."

"Me, too."

"Let's go to lunch and celebrate. Mom and Dad wanted to take us out anyway. How about it, Eric? Can you come with the notorious Harcourts?"

She was teasing but Eric detected the embarrassment behind the comment. Barnaby Harcourt had hurt his own family as well as many others.

With regret, he shook his head. "Wish I could. But I have a meeting in five minutes."

Sam said, "Me, too, Ashley. In fact, the meeting was my idea and it's really important."

Ashley looked more curious than disappointed. "Well, okay. I'll meet you back at the house later. We'll talk then. Promise?"

"Absolutely." The sisters exchanged another quick hug. After Ashley left, Sam asked, "Where are we meeting the Sharpes?"

"Caleb said we could use his office." He took her elbow and guided her up the side aisle.

"Did you tell him what's going on?"

"Not in detail. Only that we suspected a problem

and wanted to apprise the parents. Don't worry. Caleb is discreet. Ministers have to be or no one will talk to them."

They made their way through the departing congregation stopping here and there to say hello. By the time they reached the church offices, the Sharpes were coming down the opposite hall.

In their forties, both Ed and Janet Sharpe were tall like their daughter, though Eric was certain he'd heard Gina was adopted. A curly redhead, Janet carried a few extra pounds and wore bifocals. Ed was a slender man with receding brown hair.

After greeting the pair, Eric opened Caleb's office door and allowed the others to go inside first. He was glad to see Caleb had made sure there were enough chairs. "Everyone, have a seat."

Mr. and Mrs. Sharpe exchanged glances before sitting side by side in a pair of blue-gray padded guest chairs. Sam chose a chair across from them. Eric dragged Caleb's computer chair around the desk to sit closer to the couple. As a missionary, he'd always been the hands-on type, believing that proximity denoted personal interest. He not only wanted the Sharpes to feel comfortable but also to believe his sincerity.

"Ed. Janet. Thanks for meeting with us."

"You said it was about Gina," Mrs. Sharpe said, her expression tense. "Is something wrong?"

No use beating around the bush. He'd known the Sharpes since first attending Chestnut Grove Community Church a year ago and knew them to be decent, hardworking people. Ed was a diesel mechanic who worked long hours and Janet worked part-time in one of the area museums.

"We think there is. Are you familiar with anorexia?"

"The eating disorder movie stars get?"

"Not just movie stars, Mrs. Sharpe," Sam said, leaning forward. Her long blond hair tumbled over one shoulder. "Unfortunately, a lot of teenage girls get it, too."

Ed frowned. "Are you saying Gina has anorexia?"

"We think so. Eric and I have both spent a lot of time with Gina lately. Something is definitely not right. She seldom eats and when she does it's salad."

"There's nothing wrong with salad. It's good for her. We encourage her to eat lots of vegetables."

"What my wife means is Gina has always been thin. She's allergic to a lot of things. Heavy foods upset her stomach, so she's a picky eater. I'm sure there's nothing here to worry about."

Eric could sense Sam's anxiety rising.

"I have to disagree," she said. "In my business I've encountered plenty of eating disorders and Gina has all the symptoms."

Janet Sharpe bristled. "At the risk of being argumentative, Miss Harcourt, anorexia may be common in your business, but this is Chestnut Grove. Girls around here have more sense."

"It's happening all over America, Janet," Eric put in. "I don't know as much about this as Sam does, but I've been researching. Most teenage girls diet at some point, but girls with a distorted body image take dieting to the extreme."

"I understand that, but Gina is an honor student. She's brilliant. She plays the piano and takes ballet. She has friends and dates a nice boy. She's active in church and does volunteer work. There is nothing distorted about our daughter."

"Unfortunately, most girls who develop anorexia are high achievers like Gina. Girls who've developed unrealistic expectations." Girls like Sam, he thought.

"But we've tried to give Gina every opportunity. We encourage her to excel because she can, but we've never forced her to do anything more," Ed said. "We're proud of her grades and her talents."

"And you have a right to be. But somewhere something went awry and she began to crumble beneath the pressure."

"We appreciate your concern, Eric, but I'm a good mother. I'd know if my child had a problem." Janet Sharpe rose and gathered her purse. "We really need to go now. We have company coming this afternoon."

Her husband rose, too.

Eric's heart sank. This was not going the way he'd hoped.

Gray eyes worried, Sam stood and laid elegant fingers on Janet's arm. "I'm sure you're a great mom, and we're not trying to offend you. We're just worried about Gina. She's a great girl. Please keep an eye on her and let us know if you notice anything at all. Will you do that much?"

The woman's stiffness eased. "Of course we will. Gina is our whole life. She's our only child."

Eric extracted his wallet and took out a business card. "Give me a call if we can help."

Without hesitation, Ed took the card, then offered his other hand for Eric to shake. "We appreciate your concern, Eric. Thanks, anyway."

And then the couple departed, leaving Sam and Eric staring at the closed office door.

"That went well," Eric said lightly.

"Not." Sam pushed both hands up the back of her head, lifting her hair in a gesture he'd seen her do a dozen times. Though certain the move was a modeling pose, it was so feminine and uncontrived, Eric wished she'd do it again.

"Maybe we approached them the wrong way. They seemed defensive as if we were accusing them of bad parenting."

"Well, think about it. Maybe they feel insecure because Gina's adopted."

"Nothing we can do now except try to talk to Gina again and pray something we say to her or in Sunday school will make a difference."

"That's not good enough," Sam insisted. "She needs help immediately."

"Any suggestions?"

"None." In agitation, Sam pressed her fingertips to both temples. "I'm scared for her, Eric."

"I know you are." And he admired Sam more every minute. The woman he'd believed to be shallow was deeply compassionate. "How about if we brainstorm ideas over lunch? The Starlight makes terrific Sunday fried chicken."

"*Fried* chicken?" Sam pretended horror. "You're trying to cost me my job. I never eat fried *any*thing."

"Live dangerously. We can always go for a run later."

He looped an arm over her shoulders, keeping the action as casual as possible.

Regardless of the inner warnings against a personal relationship with Sam, Eric figured they were too late. A week ago, he'd almost kissed her. Maybe he'd get another chance today.

As soon as the idea came, guilt followed. Gina was in serious trouble and all he could think of was kissing Sam.

Disappointed in himself, he let his arm slide from Samantha's shoulders.

Chapter Nine

Sam was trapped.

The doorbell rang again for at least the twentieth time, but she didn't race down the stairs. She knew who it was.

Reporters.

She gazed out the window of her temporary bedroom to the chaotic scene below. A half-dozen media types camped outside the Harcourt mansion waiting for her appearance. She'd opened the door once, but not again. Not after the horrible things they'd said.

The telephone jangled. She didn't dare answer.

She picked up the *Richmond Gazette* and read the piece again. The paper had received another letter, full of poisonous threats and accusations toward the ongoing investigation at the Tiny Blessings Adoption Agency.

This time, the author specifically mentioned the

Harcourt family, spewing veiled accusations, claiming the living Harcourts were as guilty as the dead Barnaby Harcourt. At one point, the writer stated, "The Harcourts, especially Samantha the fancy model, have an inflated sense of self-importance." The letter writer went on to rehash Ashley's child born out of wedlock and hinted that Sam must be hiding some indiscretion to have remained in provincial Chestnut Grove for such an extended period of time.

As intended, the words stung. And had set the tabloids on fire with speculation.

Ever since Ross Van Zandt had begun his probe of the records, trouble had followed like hungry hyenas stalking a wounded antelope.

Though she and her family were no longer directly connected with the agency or the investigation, they couldn't escape the past. After the recent discovery of Ben Cavanaugh's false adoption papers in her wall, the pressure had mounted. Her grandfather had left behind a terrible legacy of lies, extortion and baby selling.

As a result, any number of people could be uncomfortable with Ross's investigation, as well as with the stories in the *Gazette* and other less reputable papers. Jared Kierney, an honest reporter who had adopted through Tiny Blessings, was doing his best to show the agency in a positive light. He had also gone out of his way to de-vilify the remaining Harcourt family.

Unfortunately, it wasn't working. At least not today. For whatever reason, someone wanted an end to the investigation and news reports. And they weren't afraid to send scathing letters to both the agency and the newspaper. Letters that fueled a ravenous media.

Yellow journalism prevailed, especially when a spokesmodel and her wealthy family were involved. Even her agent had heard the news and worried Style would pull her contract due to negative publicity.

A band of tension squeezed her forehead. She rubbed at it.

"Lord, if you're available, I sure could use some peace and quiet."

Someone pounded on the front door. Though she should be immune by now, Sam jumped. She doubted seriously it was the help she'd prayed for.

"Miss Harcourt. Give us a statement."

Yeah, right. They didn't want a statement. They wanted something scandalous or scintillating, especially if they could stick her picture above a misleading caption. Though she maintained a low profile, being the Style girl made her a target for every bozo with a camera and a hankering to make a few bucks.

The phone jangled again. Fed up, she stormed across the room and turned off the ringer. "Why didn't I do that an hour ago?"

A moment later, her cell phone rang. She flinched, wishing she hadn't given her card to every kid in the Sunday school class. Surely, none had shared with a reporter. She grabbed for it, checking the caller ID.

Eric. A bubble of pleasure followed the relief. "Thank goodness it's you."

"I'd like to take that as a compliment, as if you

were waiting beside the phone, longing for my call. Considering the scene down here this morning, and the fact that I have a volunteer whose only job today is to deal with the media, I don't think that's what you meant."

"It wasn't, although I'm really, really glad to hear from you. This place is a circus."

"Figured as much. Reporters?"

"Everywhere. I can't imagine how they got through the gates, but they did."

"Unscrupulous paparazzi have ways we can't even imagine." His baritone was a pleasant burr in her ear. "They've been here, too, but Ross sent them packing. He was furious, worrying about the stress on Kelly."

"He should be. It's awful. I'm a prisoner in my own house."

"You're not there alone, are you?"

"Yes, unfortunately. Ashley didn't have class so she headed up to Williamsburg to see her fiancé. Dad and Mother drove into Richmond for the day to see Aunt Sharon."

"Why didn't you go?"

"I had some errands to run, calls to return, business stuff, but there is no way I can do those now. I called Mother and Dad and warned them to stay in Richmond tonight. Until this dies down, I'm trapped."

"I guess that rules out lunch, huh?"

"Afraid so." But she was delighted he'd asked.

"Can't you sneak out, meet me somewhere?"

"Are you kidding?" She shoved her hair back in

frustration. "These piranha are watching every door and window."

"I don't like the sound of that." She could practically see the worried V between his eyebrows. "We need to get you out of there."

"If there is a way, I don't know what it is."

The line was quiet for several seconds. Only his soft breathing assured her the call had not been dropped.

"Give me a few minutes to think of something and to make a few calls," he said. "I might have an idea. I'll call you back. Stay safe and don't answer the door. Okay?"

"Absolutely."

Safe. She hadn't considered the possibility of danger. To what lengths would the paparazzi go?

Even though she and Eric had accomplished exactly nothing, she felt better, calmer. She pushed the end button and snapped the cell phone closed. During the next fifteen minutes, the doorbell rang over and over again. She tried to tune it out, but her nerves now jumped at every sound. If reporters could breach the gate, who was to say they couldn't get inside the mansion?

When her cell chirped, she wilted with relief. She had no idea what Eric could do but he served as a friendly distraction and made her feel safe.

"Eric?" she said into the mouthpiece.

"Yep. Me. Your gardener is coming over. Where is the best place for him to park?"

"My gardener?" She frowned, trying to follow his drift. "Albert knows where to go."

"Humor me."

"Okay." What was Eric up to? "At the side entrance in front of the back security gate."

She went to the window overlooking the front lawn and peeked through the drapes. To her horror, a satellite truck rumbled down the drive.

"When you see his van, be prepared to let him in. Watch for a signal."

"Eric, what's going on? What are you up to?"

But the line went silent. She stared at the dead phone for a second and then smiled.

Eric was up to something, all right. What had he done? Convinced Albert to sneak her out? As goofy as the idea was, it tickled her. Some of her tension evaporated. Leave it to Eric to turn a nerve-racking event into an adventure.

Fueled by a surge of unexpected energy, Sam trotted down the stairs to the side entrance, careful to remain away from the windows.

By the time the familiar white van bearing Albert's insignia arrived, Sam was ready to do battle. She'd much rather stand and fight than hide. Outwitting a mob of harassing reporters was right up her alley.

She peered through the security peephole as three reporters came around the side of the house toward the gardening van. The driver popped out, tool tote in hand, and headed for the side entrance.

Sam squinted at the dark figure. Albert was short, stocky and Hispanic. Though dressed in gardener's overalls and sporting a ball cap, the man coming toward her was none of those things.

She sucked in a gasp of surprise.

"Eric," she whispered. "You crazy man."

One of the reporters called out. "Sir. Hold up. A couple of questions please."

"*¿Qué?*" The gardener turned slightly, expression puzzled.

"What's your name? Do you work for the Harcourts?"

"*¿Qué?*" Eric said again.

Exasperated, the reporter spoke very slowly. "Are you the gardener? Did you work for Barnaby Harcourt?"

Eric waved his hand and batted his eyes in total confusion. "*No comprendo. Español. No comprendo.*"

The three reporters looked at each other, suspicious but uncertain.

By now, Eric had reached the back steps. The newsmen waited expectantly, gaze fixated on the door, but instead of knocking, Eric stared straight at the peephole and winked. Then he whipped a pair of sheers from the tool tote and began whacking her mother's favorite verbena. A tuneless whistle erupted from his lips.

Sam clamped a hand over her mouth and giggled.

The reporters watched for a few minutes, eyeing the gardener with suspicion. Eric ignored them. He just kept whacking away at the bush as if he knew what he was doing. Someone snapped his picture. He looked up, grinned a big, goofy grin, waved his sheers and went merrily back to whacking.

Mother would not be happy about this.

And the notion made Sam laugh all the harder.

About that time a motor sounded around front. Car doors slammed. The interlopers shot Eric one last glance, then rushed away, leaving the incommunicative gardener to his work.

When they had cleared the corner of the house, Eric sprang into action, tossed the sheers into the tote and signaled Sam to open the door. As soon as he slipped inside and flipped the lock behind him, Sam slid to the floor in a fit of giggles.

"You have the worst Mexican accent I have ever heard."

White teeth flashed. He whipped off his hat and bowed. "What? You don't appreciate my fine acting talents?"

"Actually, I do. I haven't laughed so much since the picnic. Mother will die when she sees her verbena."

"Hey! I only trimmed a little." His grin was sheepish. "Maybe a lot. Should I buy her a new one?"

Sam waved off the worry. "Albert will take care of it, although he may never forgive you for damaging one of his babies." Her giggle said it really didn't matter. "How did you manage this? And what have you done with poor Albert?"

"Poor Albert is sitting over at the Starlight Diner, drinking Sandra Lange's good coffee and counting his money."

"You rented his van?"

"I thought it was a pretty ingenious idea on such short notice." He looked proud of himself, too. Cute, cute, cute. Eric was the cutest, most fun guy she knew.

"Can't argue that. But now you're stuck in here with me," she said.

Eric shrugged. "I can think of worse things."

He set the tools on the floor and removed a pair of thick jersey gloves.

"Just wait until you've been here a while. You'll change your mind."

"That bad, huh?"

"You don't know the half of it. Come on in. I have tea and coffee in the kitchen."

She led him toward the spacious kitchen, which had been remodeled recently to incorporate all the latest gleaming stainless appliances and granite countertops. Their shoes tapped on stone tile flooring.

"Beautiful place." Eric's cheerful voice grew quiet.

"Mother's on a constant remodeling kick. Every time I come home something has been redone." She could almost read his thoughts. "I know the money could be better spent."

"I didn't say that."

"But you were thinking it and you're right. The money belongs to them, though, and I'm trying to stop feeling guilty about the things I can't control." Like the bagel and cream cheese she'd had for breakfast. She reached into a glass-front cabinet and took down two frosted glasses. "Tea?"

"No, thanks."

"I have to give you something for coming to my rescue."

"You aren't rescued yet." His grin was back. He wiggled his eyebrows. "But I'm plotting."

The doorbell rang again, one long ring as if someone leaned on it. He gave it an annoyed glance.

"Has this been going on all morning?"

Sam nodded morosely. "Awful, isn't it?"

"That would drive anybody crazy. We have to get you out of here."

She shrugged. "Reporters will show up anywhere we go."

"True." Deep in thought, Eric stared at the microwave as though it held the mysteries of the universe. Eyes dancing, he pointed at her. "Wait a minute. I know of one place where no one would ever think of looking."

"Where? Mars?" Since landing the Style Fashions campaign, Sam had never found any place to be private from the media. And she had long since discovered, the more she complained, the more attention she garnered.

"Better than Mars. A place with AC, plenty of snacks *and* a plasma screen." Looking pleased, he tapped himself on the chest. "My place. We can hide out, cook lunch, watch a little TV, play with Barker. It'll be great."

"Barker?"

"My dog."

"You own a dog?"

Eric shook his head in mock sadness. "He owns me. Big, shaggy and in total control. What do you say? You game?"

She'd never seen his house, but she loved the idea. Anywhere was better than here. Being with Eric was best of all. "Sure, but how do we get past the piranha?"

Eric pumped dark eyebrows. "Ve vill find a vay."

Sam laughed. "You sound like the villain in an old movie."

"You don't like my disguise?" Eric pretended offense.

"I love it." Regardless of his earlier refusal, Sam took down two glasses, setting them on the counter with a soft clink. "It got you inside the house."

"And now it will get us both out. Time to put my diabolical plan into motion."

Glasses in hand, Sam crossed to the refrigerator for ice. "And what plan would this be?"

"The one I am devising as we speak. You need a disguise. A real dandy one like mine."

She was tempted to roll her eyes, but his disguise had worked. What harm was there in trying? No matter what happened, it would be fun to play along. The distraction alone was worth the effort.

"Well, let's see. My sister used to wear wigs quite a bit. I could probably find one. She won't mind."

"Perfect. But we need more. Anyone in his right mind is going to recognize someone as beautiful as you. Unless…"

Sam didn't miss the compliment, finding it all the sweeter because Eric gave it so matter-of-factly. "Unless what?"

She set the glasses on the counter and scrounged around for the sugar bowl. She hadn't used sugar in so long, she'd forgotten what the bowl even looked like, but like a good Southern boy, Eric took his tea sweet. Really, really sweet.

"Unless," Eric went on thinking out loud, "they think you're a tall, skinny kid. A boy kid. Got any old, loose clothes that might do the trick?"

"Mr. Pellegrino, you are a devious man," she teased over one shoulder. "No wonder I like you. Are you certain you aren't an international spy?"

"If I tell you—"

"I know, I know." She raised both hands in the air, laughing at his silliness. "If you tell me, you'll have to kill me."

He feigned shock. "No way. Double-O-Seven never waxes the pretty girls. But he does take them out to dinner."

"Well, thank goodness for that." Metal clinked against glass as she stirred in the sugar. Forty-eight calories' worth. "The attic is filled with old clothes and lots of other junk. I'm sure we can find something up there."

"Excellent." He took the proffered tea and swigged deeply, the muscles of his throat flexing as he drank. Sam felt silly to be so mesmerized by a man's throat muscles.

To hide a sudden, uncommon self-consciousness, she carefully focused her gaze on Mother's china cabinet and sipped the tea. The icy coolness concealed the flush of awareness.

"That's good stuff." Eric backhanded his mouth in that intriguing male manner. "Thanks. All this espionage business creates a powerful thirst."

"Well, Mr. Bond." Sam set her glass aside and

wiped moist hands on a paper towel. "Ready to check out the attic?"

"I take it you're eager to get this show on the road." When she gave him a what-do-you-think look, he laughed, drained the last of his tea and plunked the glass on the counter. With a gallant sweep of his arm, he said, "Lead the way."

Eric followed Sam down a long hall lined with fine art and sedate color. The Harcourt Mansion was every bit as stately as the Noble Estate. Sam had grown up in the lap of luxury.

A knot formed in his belly, briefly overriding the happy conspiratorial mood. He'd never told her about his background. Would she look down her famous nose at a blue-collar boy who'd grown up fixing old cars and working odd jobs?

What was he doing here anyway?

But he knew the answer to that. At least part of it. Samantha was a new Christian. In his experience, the first days and weeks after accepting the Lord were crucial to Christian growth and keeping the faith. He'd led her to the Lord himself and as a result had a certain responsibility to her.

Ah, why was he lying to himself? Responsibility or not, he would still be here. And that worried him. Even if she wasn't the Style model with her face on every billboard and magazine, Sam's life didn't include two little orphan boys from Africa. For him, they were a gift. He didn't expect any woman to share that ideal. He'd long ago settled on being a single dad. The decision had never bothered him before.

Eric shook off the thoughts. He liked her. She liked him. They were having a good time today. No use letting his own insecurities run wild.

With light feet, Sam trotted ahead of him. A curving staircase such as the kind he'd only seen in movies took them up to the third-story attic. All the attics he'd seen were creepy places filled with dust and wires and spiders, something straight out of a horror movie. The Harcourt attic, though a bit dusty, was tidy and organized. Through a single dormer window, sunlight splashed gold along the hardwood floor.

Hands on his hips to catch his breath from the long climb, Eric gazed around. "Don't tell me the maid cleans up here."

"Occasionally. Mother has allergies." Sam's answer came in between short breaths.

"The renovations must be giving her fits."

"They are." As if he'd asked, she explained, "Remodeling a suite of rooms for me was a gift from my parents, Eric. I didn't even know about it until I arrived home a couple of months ago."

"Sorry. I was hoping you hadn't noticed my bad attitude. I know you better now." And wanted to know her even better.

Jammed with covered furniture, the attic held boxes and plastic containers of every size, several large trunks and a long rack of hanging clothes.

Eric popped the lid off several boxes, finding

Christmas decorations and a hodgepodge of home decor no longer in use.

"These on top must be the newest. Where is the older stuff?"

Sam glanced over the shoulder of a simple blue fitted T-shirt, her long dangly earrings catching the overhead light. Sam always looked pretty, but only she could turn a T-shirt and capris from ordinary to spectacular. She was too thin, but he still thought she was perfect.

The thought brought him up short. Perfect? Where had that come from? He knew better. She'd told him of her struggles with anorexia, and yet he admired her all the more because of them.

"Over in that corner, probably," she was saying. "Oh, wait a minute. I know." She moved around him, brushing close enough for Eric to catch a hint of her exotic fragrance. "There might be some of my uncle's old clothes in this trunk. He died young. An accident, of some kind, and my grandmother could never turn loose of anything that belonged to him."

Sam lifted the trunk lid.

"Well. Look at this." Her voice went quiet. "My very first outfit." As Eric peered over her shoulder, she took out a pink-and-white baby dress complete with pink shoes and bonnet. "I've seen it in pictures."

"Pretty. Your mother must be saving it for your little girl someday."

An odd look passed over Samantha's face. She dropped the outfit like a hot potato and slammed the lid. "Nothing useful in there."

She quickly moved away from the trunk toward yet another. "One of these trunks has to be the right one."

Eric followed, wondering about the abrupt reaction to her old baby clothes. She and her parents shared a once-strained, still-struggling relationship. Could that be the reason for her odd behavior?

A puff of dust wafted up as Sam raised the lid of an age-darkened trunk and lifted out a long pair of camouflage overalls. "What is this?"

"Any hunters in the family? Or military men?"

"I don't know. Probably not Uncle Joseph. He was only a teenager." She held the coveralls in front of her. "Would these work?"

"Yep." With a grin, he reached into the trunk, pulled out a ball cap and plunked it on her head. "We have to do something about your hair. It's too blond and easily recognized."

She cocked her head to one side, eyes narrowed in thought. "Ashley's wigs. And maybe a few other little makeup tricks. You go downstairs and have another glass of tea. I'll be down in a minute, ready to play—" she paused for dramatic effect and then wiggled all ten fingers toward him "—mission impossible."

He slapped her a high five. "That's what I'm talking about. Time to get the party started."

Chapter Ten

Breathless, laughing like a giddy teenager, Sam hopped up and down behind Eric as he jiggled a key in the front door of a tidy little cottage. In the long, heavy overalls she felt every bit of the ninety-plus temperature. The dappled shade of red and purple crepe myrtles flanking either side of the small wooden porch offered little respite from the stifling August heat. Regardless of the discomfort and the real threat of being followed by the scandal-hungry press, Sam was actually enjoying herself—and her companion.

With a mock scowl, Eric glanced over one shoulder. "So impatient."

Fidgety, adrenaline still pumping from the wild escape, she gave him a playful push, eager to get inside before being discovered. "Hurry."

Instead, Eric whipped around, hands raised like claws, to growl like a bear. Sam squealed and jumped away, laughing so hard she nearly tumbled backward off the porch.

With reflexes born of a good athlete, Eric caught her shoulders and yanked. The action propelled her into his sturdy chest, but Eric held steady, as close now as a whisper.

"Rescued," she murmured.

"Or captured," he replied with an ornery twinkle.

Closely matched in height, though Eric stood several inches taller, the appreciable difference in their bodies was in girth. Eric's muscled athletic frame dwarfed her lean one.

"Captured could be nice," she murmured, reluctant to move but knowing full well if they'd been followed, a reporter would spot them any moment.

A breath apart, they smiled into each other's eyes. Eric had nice eyes, sort of milk chocolate, with flecks of gold and a solid black ring around the iris. If eyes were the windows to the soul, Eric's soul was honest and kind and full of mischief.

The idea filled her with a strange sort of contentment. Here was a man she could trust and lean on and share good times.

She wanted to soak in every little detail about him. The way he looked, the way he smelled, the things he said and did. She wasn't looking for a husband but if she were…

The thought brought her up short. Like most girls, she'd always expected to find her true love some day and have a family. After her modeling career waned or when she'd stumbled on to the right guy.

But then had come the unexpected diagnosis from her doctor. Since then she'd only dated men as shallow as herself—men who were far too egocentric to share her with children.

She knew better than to get involved with a man like Eric. Yet here she was, close enough to admire the crinkled corners of his eyes and wish he would kiss her. He hovered, chest rising and falling from exertion, breath warm against her forehead. When he made no move, she tiptoed up and pressed her lips against his whisker-rough cheek.

"You're a lot of fun, Mr. Bond."

His hand went to the spot where she'd kissed him. "Wow, kissed by a girl with a beard. I'll never wash my face again."

Sam shook her head in pretend exasperation. "Are you going to open the door or stand here until that dog barks himself to death and the reporters come to find out what all the fuss is about?"

"Yes," he said, still silly and playful. But he pushed the door open and waved her inside. Happy and filled with energy, she stepped into the cool, dim living area and looked around. It was what she expected in a single man's house. Casual, comfortable, with more entertainment system than furniture. He wasn't joking about the plasma. Boy, did he ever have a television set!

Eric's dog bounded toward the entry. True to his name, Barker maintained a decibel level loud enough to scare the bravest burglar. But when Eric spoke his name, the big shaggy mongrel did a belly crawl, teeth displayed in a gratuitous grin.

"Hey, there, Barker." Sam held a tentative hand toward the animal. "I'm Sam. Don't bite me, okay?"

Barker sniffed her fingers, whined loudly and collapsed at her feet.

Eric groaned. "Come on, Barker. Have a little dignity. At least play hard to get."

Sam scratched the dog's ears and was rewarded with a contented groan. "How long have you had him?"

"Since about fifteen minutes after I moved in here. He arrived in my backyard as I unloaded my television, and no amount of searching ever turned up another owner. I think he fell for the HDTV."

"What kind is he?"

Eric shrugged. "Pure unadulterated mutt."

As if insulted, the dog leaped to his feet, shook himself, then stalked to the back door and whined. Eric pushed the door open and stuck his head out, looking left and right.

"No reporters in sight. I think we outsmarted them."

"Thank goodness. Free at last." Beneath all the coverups, her head was roasting. Sam yanked away the baseball cap and wig to shake her hair loose, relishing the rush of cool air. "I still can't believe we ditched that SUV so easily. How did you do that? What are you? A NASCAR driver masquerading as a missionary?"

"Or a mad missionary motorist masquerading as a social worker?"

"Who is masquerading as a gardener." For unfathomable reasons, Eric brought out a part of her character she'd thought lost in high school. Playful, upbeat and undeniably happy. "I'm starting to wonder who you really are."

Whipping off the broad-brimmed straw hat, he slapped it over his heart and struck a pose. "I am a man of great mystery."

"Yes, it's a mystery we escaped my house. It's also a mystery how anyone was fooled by that awful disguise."

"Hey, don't go dissing my disguise again. I think it adds an air of mystery and romance."

"Oh, definitely. Very romantic. I nearly swooned at the sight."

"Swooned, huh?" Eyes dancing merrily, he said, "Cool. Very cool. You hungry?"

"Starving." A truth that surprised her. "Pretending to be an international spy whets the appetite."

"Good. I grill a mean steak if you're up to living dangerously."

Her taste buds went on red alert while an internal calorie counter flashed numbers through her head faster than a Vegas slot machine gone wild. "Steak? As in beef?"

"No, silly. Steak as in green beans." When she laughed, he said, "Hey, I'm a Texas boy. We eat beef. Lots and lots of beef."

He tossed his gardening hat on a chair and moved toward a doorway.

"Texas, huh?" She tossed her cap and wig on the same chair and followed. "I've heard about you Texas men."

"Yeah? Well, it's all true," he said. "Whatever you heard."

"Let's see. Macho. Arrogant. Stubborn."

"Yep. That's us."

Sam didn't believe a word of it. Eric was all man, but he wasn't stubborn or arrogant. Not after he'd quickly apologized for misjudging her.

She followed him into the kitchen, a sunny yellow, country-style room with white tile and cabinets, and bright curtains at the double windows. "What a great kitchen."

Eric took two steaks from the freezer and tossed them into the microwave. "The ladies at the agency helped me paint when I first moved here. The curtains were Anne's touch. Kelly chose the yellow. Being a wise man with two sisters, I know the power of women on a decorating mission. I kept my mouth shut and let them have their way."

"Do you like it?"

"Love it. I offered to let them do the rest of the house, but they disappeared on me after that."

"What's left to do? Everything looks nice to me."

She supposed that sounded false coming from someone who grew up in a nine-bedroom mansion and owned a condo this cottage would fit in, but she was truthful. There was something warm and inviting about Eric's place.

"The boys' room mainly. I can't decide what to do with it."

"Matunde and Amani? I could help you, if you'd like."

He turned serious eyes toward her. "Would you?"

"I'd love doing that. And if you'd let me, I'd like to send them packages, gifts, little things to encourage them until they come home."

"If they ever do."

This morning he'd spent an hour on the telephone wrangling with government officials in Johannesburg. International adoption was in constant flux; one day the news was good and the next he wondered if Amani and Matunde would ever come home to him. Even though they were well cared for in the orphanage, he missed the boys and knew they wondered why he hadn't come to get them as promised.

"Don't lose faith, Eric." Not that she knew much about faith yet, but the more time she spent with Eric, the more she learned.

"You're right. And the boys are crazy about getting little packages. Just don't overdo and spoil them. I can't keep up with your credit card."

The words were spoken lightly, but Sam heard the concern behind them. Her money intimidated a lot of people. She was disappointed to know Eric was one of them.

The microwave beeped. Sam reached around and took the steaks out, gently pushing Eric out of the way. She wasn't a cook, but she wasn't helpless in the kitchen, either.

Feeling uncharacteristically domestic, she found jars of seasoning and sprinkled the meat while Eric dragged out potatoes, dishes and a loaf of Texas toast.

In the small confines, they edged around one another, brushing and bumping so that Sam was acutely aware of her companion. Tall and well-built, Eric filled the space with a masculine presence. There was something attractively male about a man and a grill and steaks. And though she was nearly as tall as Eric, Sam enjoyed feeling small and protected for a change.

The thought brought a smile.

"What are you grinning about?" Metal rattled as he dragged utensils from a drawer.

"You."

Spatula upraised, he paused. "I like the sound of that."

She didn't satisfy his curiosity. "Want me to make a salad?"

He tried to look disgusted. "Women and green stuff. Always trying to do the healthy thing when all a man wants is steak and potatoes. And maybe a hunk of bread."

She gave him a look and opened the fridge. "Aha!" she cried, whirling around with a bag of pre-packaged salad in hand. "You do eat green stuff."

His twinkling gaze slid sideways. "I think my mom must have come by."

"All the way from Texas?"

"Maybe she mailed it to me?"

By now Sam was laughing again. With Eric, she seemed to laugh all the time.

With a playful flourish intended to keep her laughing, he tossed the steaks onto the grill. The sizzling scent rose and tantalized Sam's nose.

While the steaks cooked, they leaned against the counter and talked, about the boys and the adoption, about outwitting the media and their exciting escape, about Eric's work and scandals that wouldn't die.

By the time everything was cooked and placed on the small square table, Sam's stomach gnawed with hunger. Normally, she had to make herself eat, having tuned out natural hunger pangs for so long her mind didn't recognize them. But not today. Today, whether from the adventure, the company or the food, she looked forward to the meal.

"This looks wonderful," she said honestly.

As she moved to pull out a chair, Eric stopped her. "Allow me, ma'am."

"Why, thank you, sir." She gave a little curtsy, but in truth she was pleased by the courtesy. "Do all Texas men have such good manners?"

"They do where I grew up or their mamas will hurt them."

Sam doubted very seriously Eric's mama had needed to be too stern with him. "I'll bet you were the spoiled apple of your mother's eye."

"How did you guess?" He took the chair across the table and reached toward her, palms up.

Without giving the action a second thought, Sam laid her hands in his. The rough warmth of his skin against hers sent a curious ripple along her nerve endings. She really, really liked Eric Pellegrino, and from all appearances, he felt the same. Since Sam had accepted the Lord, their friendship had grown to something more. Though she didn't like the term *boyfriend,* she wondered if he was hers.

Eric's strong fingers curled around hers and he bowed his head. Shame pricked her conscience. Here she was thinking about Eric as a man and all he wanted to do was pray.

While his voice rumbled quietly over the food, Sam said a prayer of her own thanking God to have met such a good and decent man. A man she could fall in love with if she wasn't careful.

The thought froze inside her head like paused video. Would it be wrong for her to fall in love?

She didn't know. Right now, she wanted to be with him, to laugh and feel like a normal woman. She'd worry about the other another time.

Eric watched with pleasure as Sam polished off half of a grilled-to-perfection club steak. He couldn't remember a time he'd enjoyed a woman's company this much. Sometimes she grew silent and introspective, and he wondered what she was thinking. And the thought crossed his mind that a woman who could have anyone wouldn't be interested in an ordinary Joe like him, but Sam's actions told him different.

Their escape from the reporters had been both fun and worrisome. Whoever wanted to stop the investigations was making life miserable for anyone involved with Tiny Blessings. The last person who had tried to silence the inquiry had turned out to be dangerous and insane.

"Have you ever considered that you could be in danger?" he asked when Sam mentioned the reporters again.

Laying her fork aside, she shook her head. A blond curl, in pretty disarray from wearing the wig earlier, brushed against her shoulder. "Not really. The harassment is annoying and embarrassing, but I'm not afraid, if that's what you mean."

"I wasn't here two years ago when the mayor's wife was willing to kill Kelly and anyone else to keep her husband's indiscretions quiet, but we could be dealing with another psycho."

Sam frowned and bit down on her bottom lip. Eric tried not to notice how full and pretty her mouth was.

"You don't think Gabriel and Ashley could be in danger, do you?"

He had to consider the possibility. "Maybe you should go back to Chicago. Take them with you for a while."

"Ashley's in college and has a fiancé. She won't leave."

Shooting for casual, Eric asked a question that plagued him. "What about you? You have a career to get back to anyway. Wouldn't you be safer in Chicago?"

"Trying to get rid of me?"

"Not even close. But I don't want to lose you to a psycho, either."

"Chicago holds no appeal right now. Everything I'm interested in is here in Chestnut Grove."

Unaware he'd been holding his breath, Eric

released a sigh. A man could read a lot into a statement like that. And Eric wanted to believe she meant him.

Okay, so he was falling and falling fast. He'd known this would happen if he spent much time with Sam Harcourt. Hadn't he begun to fall in love with her a year ago?

But she was the one with all the decisions to make. He wasn't about to ask her to give up a successful career for him. Even if she was discontent with modeling now, she might change her mind. He had to be ready for that to happen.

He leaned back against the spindle-backed chair and pointed at her plate. "Are you going to eat the rest of that steak or not?"

Splayed fingers pressed her midsection. "I'm stuffed. Do you want it?"

"My motto is never waste good steak." He took her plate, sliding the meat onto his.

"I don't know when I've eaten so much, but everything tasted really good."

He caught a hint of something in her voice and looked up. "You're not feeling guilty, are you? About eating, I mean."

She shook her head, pale hair moving over the shoulders of her overalls. "No."

He cocked an eyebrow at her.

She admitted, "Maybe a little, but the point is I'm eating, and the more I fight the voices in my head with the scriptures you gave me, the less I hear them."

He sliced a strip of beef and stabbed it with a fork. "I think that's a praise God, don't you?"

"Absolutely. Every day I ask Him for the grace to deal with the problem and every day I see improvement." She gnawed at her lip again. "I only wish we could help Gina in the same way."

"Have you talked to her again?"

"A couple of times. She won't let me go near the eating issue. But it's there, waiting to take her health and maybe her life. It scares me so badly."

The worry on her face was real. Sam knew, far better than he did, the kind of danger Gina faced.

"I'm praying for her every day," Eric said. "Praying for a door to open so we can help." Sometimes prayer didn't seem like enough, but he knew God had a lot more power than he ever would.

He polished off the last of Sam's leftover and pushed back his plate. "Man, that was good. Now if the maid would only show up and wash the dishes."

Sam's chair scraped against the tile floor. "I'll do them."

He stopped her with a hand on her arm. "Guests don't do dishes."

"Says who?"

"Says my mama who would have my hide if she knew."

Sam's eyes twinkled like silver lights. "Who's going to tell her?"

With a laugh, Eric started gathering the few dishes. "Not me."

As they worked side by side, Sam said, "Tell me about your family. They must be great."

"The best." Turning the taps, he ran water in the sink. "Big, rambunctious, loving."

"Brothers and sisters?"

"Two sisters, two brothers. Mom and Dad, of course, and I still have three of my grandparents, plus a host of aunts and uncles."

"Five kids?"

"Yep. I'm the baby boy."

"You miss them?" She reached under the cabinet for dishwashing liquid and squirted a healthy amount into the rushing water. White, airy bubbles filled the room with a lemony fragrance.

"Sure, but not like I once did. After working in Thailand and Africa for so many years, the kids there became my family. But Mom and the siblings came here to Virginia when I first moved in. And I always try to get home for major holidays. That's a wild and crazy time if ever there was one."

"Knowing you, I can believe that." Her lips curved a tiny bit. "Harcourt holidays have always been so…correct."

The sad admission touched Eric. Sam had no idea what she'd missed.

"When I was a little girl, I watched those Christmas specials about big, loving families and wished mine was like that."

Maybe she did know what she'd missed.

From what she'd told him, relationships within the Harcourt family had improved greatly in the last couple of years, but a childhood of cool detachment couldn't be erased.

"When you have your own kids, you can do it your way," he said. "Wild and crazy or calm and correct. Whatever you choose."

"What about you? What would you choose?"

"The same kind of childhood I had," he said. "We didn't have a lot of money or stuff, but we had love and laughter and each other."

The truth of that statement hit him between the eyes. He'd often resented being the kid who ran a paper route and mowed lawns to pay for his school clothes, but Sam's situation opened his eyes to how blessed he'd always been.

"They sound terrific." He heard the pensive note. "I would love to have a family like that."

"I was a very blessed boy, though I didn't know it then. Someday, I'll do it all over again. Ten or twelve kids, a big yard, a rambling old house in the country, ten horses, eighteen dogs, twenty-seven cats, the works."

She giggled. "Ten or twelve kids!"

He laughed, too. "Maybe not that many, but as many as my wife will agree to. Matunde and Amani are just the start. Life is more fun with a houseful of kids and noise."

"So you're planning on getting married someday?"

Hands dripping suds, he tapped Sam's nose and said, "Gotta have a wife to have all those kids."

According to the African government, he needed a wife now, a worry that he didn't share with Sam. The adoption committee continued to balk at his single status even though he'd cared for an orphanage full of children by himself for several years.

He looked at the beautiful woman drying his dishes. Emotion bubbled up inside him like suds in the sink. Something was happening between them. He was certain of that, though it was too early to know where it would lead. Still, he'd had Sam in his heart for more than a year. He couldn't help but wonder.

"Sam?" he started.

She took a dish from the sink and placed it in the drainer. "What? You look serious."

"I am. Very." He turned toward her and waited, trying to read her feelings. She gazed back, waiting, too. And he decided now was a good time to find out if they were traveling in the same direction.

He took her shoulders and very slowly pulled her to him.

"Sam?"

"You said that already."

He gave a little laugh. "I want to kiss you."

Her bow mouth lifted, and she surprised him by saying, "It's about time."

So he did. And the sweet emotion flowing out of her gave him the courage he needed.

"I care about you, Sam," he said, lips grazing hers.

She touched his cheek, and he didn't even mind the warm dampness from the dishes. "I know. I feel the same."

With a relieved sigh, he kissed her again, all the while his mind raced.

It would take a unique woman to be his wife and a mother to his children. Most women wouldn't be willing. Would Sam?

Chapter Eleven

Kids. He wanted kids. Lots of them.

The familiar feeling of despair, as heavy as an elephant, pushed down on Sam as she rifled through her closet in search of the perfect outfit to wear to the Cavanaughs' baby dedication. No matter what she did or where she went, Sam couldn't seem to escape the constant reminder of children.

Since the lunch date at Eric's house, she had thought of little else. And now the baby dedication. In truth, she was falling in love with Eric Pellegrino. And he wanted kids. Not just the two he was adopting, but biological children, as well. Who didn't?

She wanted the same thing.

With a sad sigh, she plopped down on the bed in her newly renovated suite. Mother and Dad had gone overboard, as usual, but the result was lovely. Surrounded by blues and creams, her mask collection decorated one wall and set the tone of the entire room. She'd added other pieces from her travels, giving the suite an exotic feel that she loved. The African ceremonial mask, procured by her driver, was now her favorite. Every time she gazed at the carved mahogany face, she remembered that beautiful day with Eric and his children.

The thought hurt. Eric and his children. He was made to be a dad, not to one or two but to as many as he chose. Eric would be a great dad, the kind of father every child should have.

Back in the enormous walk-in closet, she pressed the button and set the clothes racks into rotation. Plastic crinkled as the bag-encased outfits slowly spun past.

The kiss had changed everything. He cared for her. She cared for him. Their relationship was moving forward normally. Only she knew there was something abnormal that could ruin everything.

Maybe it was time to go back to her doctor and find out for sure. Dr. Smythe had said there was a chance she could conceive if she kept her weight up and took care of herself. An outside chance, but at this point, hope was all she had. But she was also afraid. What if the verdict erased that ray of hope forever?

A pale silver-blue dress caught her attention. Eric always commented when she wore blue. She pulled the dress from the rack and held it up, feeling ashamed not to even remember buying the expensive garment. How many things did she own that had been bought on a whim, never to be thought of again?

Taking great pains to look her best, Sam turned this way and that in the mirror. She'd put on a few pounds since coming back to Chestnut Grove. And that alone brought on a quivery, anxious sensation and a barrage of negative thoughts. She shouldn't have eaten the steak at Eric's. If she had time, she'd get on the treadmill for a couple more hours.

Fighting off the obsession with a prayer and a determined mind, she dressed and went downstairs to await Eric. After lunch the other day, he'd asked her to attend baby Joseph Cavanaugh's dedication with him. The entire congregation of Chestnut Grove Community had been invited, so she'd agreed.

Ben Cavanaugh had helped renovate this room, and she'd become acquainted with his wife, Leah, at church. A sprite of a woman with more energy than the famous bunny, Leah Cavanaugh had gone out of her way to make Sam feel comfortable among her new Christian friends. How could she not attend her baby boy's special day?

At the sight of Eric's vehicle coming down the drive, Sam's heart somersaulted. Amused by her own behavior, she shook her head and gave a wry chuckle. One minute, he scared her to pieces with his talk of kids and the next she couldn't wait to see him.

Giddy as a teenager she went out to meet her missionary.

The church was, as expected, packed. Most of Eric's colleagues from the agency were in attendance, as well as a large contingent of church parishioners. Already up front, Ben and Leah Cavanaugh with their daughter, Olivia, and new son waited with Reverend Fraser. Above his clerical collar, the kindly, well-loved minister glowed with happiness at the occasion. Everyone knew Reverend Fraser enjoyed baby dedications.

Program in hand, Eric gazed around at the now-familiar faces. He'd expected to see Ben's brother, Eli, at his side, but the pediatrician was conspicuously missing. Eric hoped everything was all right with Rachel. She was still on bed rest, battling preeclampsia.

"Where would you like to sit?" he murmured against Sam's flower-scented ear.

She pointed, a simple, elegant movement that sent one silver bracelet sliding along her wrist.

"Is that a space behind the Nobles? Next to Anne and Caleb?"

Tall and dark Andrew Noble, the philanthropist, sat with his fiancée, Miranda, and her son, Daniel. During the time Ross and Andrew had worked to unravel Daniel's adoption records, Eric had gained great respect for both men. Andrew might be a rich man born with a silver spoon, but he'd dedicated his life to helping others. Another reason for Eric to regret his stereotypical attitude toward all the rich.

Fingers against the silky material at Sam's back, he guided her down the aisle and squeezed in beside Anne and Caleb.

Eric and Sam exchanged smiles, nods and murmured hellos all around them. Soft music began to play, and then a hush moved over the sanctuary as Reverend Fraser stepped forward to begin the service.

"Today is the day that Lord hath made. Let us rejoice and be glad in it. And today we have a very good reason to rejoice."

He paused to smile at the bundle in Leah's arms. She and daughter Olivia beamed back while Ben looked nervous and uncomfortable in a suit and tie. Eric felt for him.

"Today," the pastor went on, "we have the privilege and joy of witnessing the public dedication of Joseph Cavanaugh. Following the example of devout parents of the Bible, Ben and Leah have expressed their desire to present Joseph to the Lord. This dedication doesn't require a sacrifice like Abraham's who was willing to place his son on an altar or even that of Hannah who dedicated her child to serve in the temple. However, it is a solemn commitment to properly care for that which God has given.

"I have had the pleasure of counseling with Ben and Leah about the responsibility of parents to raise their children in the nurture and admonition of the Lord. We've spent a number of hours searching the scripture in preparation, not just for today's service, but to better equip them for the crucial work of Godly parenting. It's my determination that both Ben and Leah and big sister, Olivia, are sincere in their desire to provide Joseph with a loving, Christ-centered upbringing."

The minister continued with the service, reading scriptures that focused on child rearing. Eric's mind wandered, though not far. Before his death, Butu, Amani and Matunde's father, had dedicated his sons, comforted by his new faith that God would provide for the boys he was leaving behind. Eric felt that responsibility and embraced it. The service had been simpler than this one, and attended by only a handful of believers, including Eric. Butu had raised tiny Matunde high over his head as an offering to God. Then he'd repeated the offering and a heartfelt prayer with three-year-old Amani, though Butu's arms trembled with weakness from the ravages of disease.

Emotion clogged the back of Eric's throat. Today's dedication was beautiful, and someday he'd dedicate his other children in a similar manner, but the service in Africa was imprinted on his heart like a brand.

Sentimental tears gathered in Sam's eyes. She blinked rapidly to disperse them and save her makeup. The heartfelt ceremony of love moved her deeply. Up front, Leah and Ben repeated vows as solemn and as precious as wedding vows. Olivia, a nine-year-old bundle of energy dressed in lavender satin, looked prouder than anyone. A loving, perfect family made even better by the addition of a son.

Without conscious decision, Sam leaned closer to Eric, his sturdy, strong shoulder a good place to lean. He glanced at her, winked and took her hand.

Sam's heart tap-danced. Holding hands with Eric felt right as together they watched the Cavanaugh family dedicate their child, their lives to the service of the Lord.

She wanted this. More than the Style campaign. More than another trip to Paris. More than anything. She wanted a family like Leah and Ben's. She wanted a husband and a baby. She wanted Eric.

"Jesus," Reverend Fraser was saying, "demonstrated His acceptance and love for the little children when He said, 'Suffer the little children to come unto me, and forbid them not: for of such is the kingdom of God.' And He took them up in His arms, put His hands upon them, and blessed them."

He took the baby from Leah's arms and held him toward the congregation. "Let us pray."

The kindly pastor prayed a sweet prayer of blessing over Joseph and his family. When he finished, the parents moved to a small lace-covered table to light a symbolic candle.

To add to the sweetness of the moment, Olivia stepped up to the microphone and began to sing. In her pure child's voice, she warbled, "Jesus Loves the Little Children" accompanied only by an unseen acoustic guitar.

And this time Sam didn't even try to hold back the sentimental tears.

When the precious ceremony ended, Pastor Fraser, all smiles, announced, "Ladies and gentlemen, it is with great pleasure that Chestnut Grove Community Church presents little Joseph Cavanaugh and his family with a dedication certificate marking this holy occasion."

Scott Crosby came forward with the certificate. During his presentation, the assistant pastor whispered something to Leah. Her wide smile grew even wider.

After the closing prayer, the effervescent Leah, with Joseph held tightly in her arms, spoke into her daughter's microphone. "Thank you all for coming. Ben and I are thrilled to have you here and we know you'll be as excited as we are to hear some wonderful news. You may have noticed that Ben's brother Eli is not here. Well..." She paused dramatically.

Her husband laughed. "What my wife is trying to say is this—Eli and Rachel are at the hospital. Rachel has just given birth to my long-awaited niece, Madeline."

Leah fairly danced up and down. "And they are both perfectly fine!"

Applause broke out and the excited buzz of voices filled the sanctuary. This was indeed good news after a long, difficult pregnancy that had threatened the life of both Rachel and her baby.

As the lighthearted crowd dismissed to the fellowship hall for a reception, Eric and Sam remained in the pew. Her hand tenderly enfolded by Eric's much larger one, Sam was reluctant to ever move.

"Nice ceremony," Eric murmured.

"Not a reporter in sight."

"Actually, there is one."

Sam's eyes widened and she glanced around. "Where's the back door?"

"Don't worry. I brought my Groucho glasses." He patted his pocket. "You can wear them if you want."

"I have my own, thanks." When he laughed as she'd intended, Sam went on. "Are there really reporters here?"

"Only one, and he's a good guy." He nodded toward the foyer where Jared Kierney and his lovely red-haired wife, Meg, stood talking to Andrew Noble. Zach Fletcher and Pilar, his expectant wife and Eric's co-worker, joined them. From their intent expressions, the conversation was serious.

Sam found Andrew Noble to be an interesting though rather mysterious man. She'd heard rumors that he was involved in some sort of clandestine rescue operations, but those stories had never been substantiated. Still, his dark looks and suave demeanor turned many heads.

But only one man turned Sam's head. And she was reluctant to ever let go of his hand.

The Kierneys' identical twin boys, dressed in matching suits, played a controlled game of touch tag with Miranda's son, Daniel, while the adults chatted. Sam fully expected the three little boys to break loose any minute and cause a commotion. From all indications, the boys had sat still as long as they could.

"I think those little guys are about to explode."

Eric rose and pulled her up, still holding her hand. "What say we go rescue them?"

"How?"

"Cake. All boys love cake." He patted his very flat stomach and for once she didn't think of her own. "Even big boys."

Together they maneuvered through the mass of humanity toward the Kierneys but the twins had dashed off toward the reception, their mother in hot pursuit.

"You've got your hands full," Sam said to Jared.

"Tell me about it." The reporter gazed fondly after his little family. "And I wouldn't have it any other way."

Sam kept her smile in place. The tender ceremony had aroused so many emotions: joy, sorrow, tenderness. She didn't know a person could be happy and sad at the same time, but she was.

Eric tugged on her hand. "Are we going for that cake or not?"

"Better hurry before my boys wipe it out." Jared grinned, falling into step beside them.

Inside the fellowship hall, an impromptu receiving line formed in front of the Cavanaughs. Some wise soul had pushed chairs together so the little family could sit and be admired. With a motherly smile, Leah placed baby Joseph in Olivia's arms.

As Sam and Eric approached to offer their congratulations, someone asked who the baby was named for.

Leah said, "Joseph is a biblical name. It means, 'God will increase.'" She slid a sly grin toward her husband. "So I'm thinking he and Olivia are only the beginning."

Ben laughed. "There's no more room in the house."

"Ah, but you're a carpenter," Leah teased. "We can build on."

During the loving exchange, Sam watched Eric

instead of the Cavanaughs and saw yearning in his eyes. Was that same longing present on her face? A longing that would likely never be fulfilled?

She shook away the thought, determined to rejoice in the Cavanaughs' special day. Resolute, she stooped to look at the new baby. In the back of her mind, she wondered if Ben would resent her presence. After all, a Harcourt was to blame for his current dilemma of discovering a birth family he hadn't known existed.

"Your brother is very handsome, Olivia," she said to the little girl.

"Thank you." Olivia gazed down at her sleeping brother. "Sometimes he stinks, and he cries too much, but I like him. Mom says we might adopt some more kids sometime. I'm adopted," she said with candor.

"Which makes you a very special little girl." Sam aimed a thumb toward Eric. "Eric is in the process of adopting two boys through the new international program at Tiny Blessings."

"International adoption?" Leah asked with interest. "That might be something Ben and I could do some day."

"*Someday* being the operative word," Ben said. "We have our hands full right now."

His eyes flickered in Sam's direction and she saw her opportunity. Clearing her throat, she said, "Ben, at the risk of bad timing, I want to apologize."

The carpenter frowned. "Apologize?"

"Yes. For the adoption records found in my home. My grandfather's deceit." The newspaper was filled with the ugliness, though Jared's series concentrated on the human aspect. Lately, he'd been chronicling Ben's story.

The new dad waved away the comment. "Not your fault. At least I know the truth now."

"Ben's planning a trip to Maryland to meet his birth family," Leah offered as she absently stroked a finger over her baby's dark fuzzy hair.

"Really?" Sam found the prospect intriguing. Maybe some good could come out of the latest revelations. "Have you been in contact with them?"

Ben nodded, but couldn't get a word in before his wife broke in. "Jared's series in the *Gazette* helped open up the lines of communication."

"Did I hear someone mention my name?" Jared, accompanied by Ross and Kelly Van Zandt, wandered into the conversation.

"We were just talking about Tiny Blessings," Eric said. "Any more ugly letters to the editor?"

Jared and the Van Zandts exchanged looks. "Not to the editor. To Kelly."

Eric reacted with shocked anger. "At the agency?"

Ross's nostrils flared. "At home. Without a stamp. Someone dropped the letter in our box as easy as you please. I've asked every neighbor if they saw anything suspicious."

"Nothing?" Eric asked, worried, too.

Ross shook his head. "Things are heating up. Somebody either blames Kelly for something that occurred at the agency or they're using her as a means to vent their anger. Either way, it ticks me off."

Eric sympathized. He'd felt the same annoyance at the press for harassing Sam. And Ross had an added concern. No man would willingly stand by and watch his pregnant wife be tormented and threatened.

Controlled anger mixed with a healthy dose of worry darkened Ross's already dark skin. "If I could get my hands on..."

"Ross," Kelly said softly, placing a hand on his arm. "Please. This is a happy day. Don't let some maniac spoil it."

"I just don't want anything happening to you." Ross tenderly touched her round belly. "Or our baby."

The love flowing between the young couple was clear for anyone to see. As happy as he was for his friends, Eric felt a tug of envy. He wanted this for himself.

Next to him Sam stood as if mesmerized by the pregnant Kelly and baby Joseph asleep in Olivia's arms. Did she feel the same pull? The same yearning to take their relationship a step further?

He reached for her hand, intending to pull her to his side. But this time, Sam quickly squeezed his fingers, then turned him loose and stepped away.

The old insecurity rushed in with a vengeance. Was Sam intentionally putting distance between them? Was their sweet time together coming to an abrupt end?

"Ready for punch?" she asked, a little too brightly.

Punch? He studied her for a moment, confused by the sudden change in her behavior.

Since when had Sam become eager to take on empty calories? Moreover, she looked spooked, like a gazelle eager to run.

Had he missed something?

Chapter Twelve

Today would change everything. One way or the other.

Sam placed a gentle kiss on Gabriel's forehead and carefully eased him into his crib. His soft blond hair lay in damp curls against his forehead where he'd lain against her shoulder for so long. Ashley no longer rocked him, but when Sam babysat, she enjoyed holding the little body close. He wouldn't be small much longer. She wanted to soak in his baby essence while she could.

Gabriel stirred, raised his head and thumped it once, twice, three times on the mattress. And then he collapsed like a rock. Sam stifled a laugh. He was such a cutie.

Tiptoeing, she left the room, closing the door with a soft snick.

As much as she loved Gabriel, he was a constant reminder of her own empty arms. Just like the baby dedication where she'd been surrounded by babies and children and pregnant women. Everywhere she looked, reminders of her childless state taunted her. And then there was Eric.

For a moment at the dedication, she'd considered breaking off their relationship. Though still undefined, she wasn't a fool. They had strong feelings for each other, whether spoken or not. Afterward, she'd prayed long and hard. Ashley claimed to get direction by praying. Sam got exactly nothing.

In the end, she'd decided to do the one thing she'd avoided for too long. She'd made the appointment with Dr. Smythe for the tests that would reveal once and for always if she could ever bear a child.

She glanced at her watch, the diamond band sparkling beneath the hall lights.

Today was D-day. Doctor day. Dr. Smythe promised to call with the results of the half-dozen medical tests. Any time now.

Her cell phone chirped. Hurrying away from the baby's door, she flipped the phone on. "Hello."

"Samantha? Dr. Smythe."

Her pulse kicked up. "What's the verdict?" No use stalling.

"As I told you during the exam, I'd really rather you come into my office for these results."

"Doctor, I appreciate your kindness, but whether here or in your office, the results are the same and I need to know now. Tell me. Can I have children?"

The pause gave Sam the answer before the physician spoke. "We don't like to use the word *never,* but Sam, it's unlikely you'll ever conceive. The damage is done. Come into my office tomorrow and we'll go over everything in detail."

Sam didn't need details. She only needed the facts.

Now inside her suite, she sat down on the bed, cradling the phone against an ear. Her heart hammered so hard, her sternum hurt. "How unlikely?"

Another pause. "At this point, very unlikely, but keep in mind, we're making strides in this area every day."

Sam rubbed shaky fingers over her eyes. She'd expected this, but hearing the verdict was hard. "What if I gain more weight? Will that help? Or maybe fertility treatments?"

"Sam." Dr. Smythe's voice gentled with compassion. "I'm sorry. Your internal organs can't take the strain. And your endocrine system malfunctioned a long time ago. But this doesn't mean you can never have a child. Today's women have babies in many ways. Adoption, surrogacy."

The kind doctor went on talking, offering counseling, urging Sam to stop by the office for more details, but Sam had already heard the most important information. Barring a miracle, she would never bear a child, the one thing she wanted most in life. She would never carry her husband's baby beneath her heart.

Eric's image flashed behind her burning eyes. For a little while she'd hoped. Eric had given her that.

Somehow she ended the call and then collapsed facedown across the silk duvet cover. She wanted to blame someone, but there was no one to blame but herself. God didn't do this. She had.

She thought of Eric again and tears gathered. Was it wrong to go on seeing him, knowing she could never have children? Was it wrong to date any man without telling him up front that she was barren? But how could a woman openly share such a personal sorrow? And when was the right time? She couldn't imagine telling a man on the first date. But wasn't it unfair to wait until feelings grew? Like now, with Eric.

She wrestled with the dilemma and found no answer.

In the room down the hall, her nephew slept on, unmindful of his aunt's despair. Little Gabriel, her sister's baby. Sam loved him so much. She was certain she would have made a wonderful mother.

Chest near to bursting, she let the tears come. And in the midst of sorrow, she turned to her new source of strength. The Lord.

After a long time of tears and prayer and self-pity, Sam lay exhausted and quiet, staring at her mask collection in thought.

A place deep inside felt empty, and she recognized it as the place that should have someday nurtured a child. She placed her hand on her stomach and for once in her life hated the perfectly flat abs. Abs that would always be flat. Always.

Barren. Such a terrible word.

And the question came again, more forceful this time.

What was she going to do about Eric?

Eric carefully hung up the telephone and stared unseeing at the photo collage on his office wall. His contact at the U.S. embassy had good news. The questions over Eric's single status appeared to be resolved and it was only a matter of time until his dossier was approved and the boys could come to America.

But a nagging sense of unease wouldn't let him go. International relations were fickle. Until Matunde and Amani landed at Richmond Airport, he wouldn't breathe easy.

He picked up the framed picture perched on his desk amid the jumble of work-related folders and messages. Amani's exuberant personality showed in his wide smile while Matunde stood shyly, head ducked in a timid grin. Eric's heart swelled with love and ached to be with the little boys he considered his own.

He took the well-worn Bible from his desk and opened it to the familiar passage in Romans.

"As many as are led by the Spirit of God, they are the sons of God. For ye have not received the spirit of bondage again to fear; but ye have received the Spirit of adoption, whereby we cry, Abba, Father. The Spirit himself beareth witness with our spirit, that we are the children of God."

The verse had become his favorite long ago and

now grew in meaning as he moved closer to adopting Matunde and Amani.

"The spirit of adoption," he murmured, rubbing his fingers across the words. God had adopted mankind, loving and providing for them with the same love He showed his biological Son. Loving the boys the way he did, Eric understood how a father could love adopted children as much as he loved his biological children.

He understood some other things, too. When a single man decided to adopt, he was making a decision that could keep him single the rest of his life. Only a very special kind of woman would be willing to mother two sons that she had neither birthed nor chosen.

Was Sam that kind of woman? Sometimes he thought she might be. At others, like in that odd moment at the reception when she'd pulled away, he wondered if she only considered him a fun date until she was ready to return to the jet set.

Today, he'd asked her to meet him for lunch. She'd behaved oddly again, but after his usual round of teasing, she'd agreed. Now that they were better acquainted, he realized she was a people pleaser. Had she said yes only to avoid hurting his feelings?

"Eric?"

At the female voice, he glanced up, surprised to find Gina hovering in the doorway.

"Gina. Hi. Come in. I didn't know you were working today." Like several of the Youth Center teens, Gina occasionally volunteered at Tiny Blessings, though from her hollow eyes the girl needed to be home in bed.

"Anne asked me to bring you these files. She said you would need them for your next appointment."

"I'd be lost without Anne," he said. "She knows what I need before I do."

With a wan smile, Gina placed the folders on his desk and turned to leave. Her shoulder blades protruded out and her arms hung like matchsticks from the sleeves of her T-shirt.

"Gina?"

Now at the door, she glanced back.

"Are you okay?"

Instantly, she straightened. Her chin shot up and a smile appeared. "Great."

"That's good." Even though it was a lie. "If you need anything..." He let the thought dwindle, having no idea what to say to a girl who was starving herself to death.

"Thanks. But Anne shows me anything I need to know."

That wasn't at all what he meant and he suspected she knew as much. Reluctant to let her leave, he said, "Did you attend the Cavanaughs' baby dedication?"

She nodded. "I went with my parents, but we had to leave early. Dad had to work." Her dark-rimmed eyes brightened momentarily. "But didn't I see you with Sam?"

No longer annoyed by the blatant matchmaking, Eric grinned. "Guilty. We had fun, too."

"Cool. So did I." Smiling, she left his office.

Eric scraped a hand over his face and leaned an elbow on the desk to say a prayer for the young girl. She was a great kid, with so much going for her. How did she get so messed up? And what was he supposed to do about it?

An hour later, the Simpkins had come and gone, pleased to have their police background clearances and agency approval to adopt a newborn. Eric crossed to the coffeepot to refill a long-empty cup. He was getting hungry but didn't take the last maple doughnut. Not with Sam coming by soon.

Since the day he'd helped her escape the reporters, he'd wanted nothing more than to spend every extra moment with beautiful Sam. Today they were trying a new Chinese restaurant in the shopping center. Though he still didn't think Sam ate enough, he would keep on feeding her. Afterward she was helping him choose decor for the boys' bedroom.

He had a few things he'd brought from Africa and others he'd picked up here and there, but Sam's opinion meant a lot. Maybe too much, all things considered.

He lifted the cup to his lips and sipped, wrestling with the question of Sam. Was he out of his mind for thinking they could be together? Some day he might go back to Africa to live. Or wherever the Lord called him. Sam wasn't exactly the missionary type.

Sure, she'd enjoyed Africa. As a tourist, a volunteer for one day. She'd never lived day in and day out with the poverty, the dirt, the heat and the lack of modern conveniences.

A high-class fashion model accustomed to limos and spas would never give that up to follow a missionary into Third World countries and be a mother to his adopted kids. Would she?

But she cared about him. She'd said as much. And she wanted a big family, same as him. Still, there was something amiss with his beautiful Sam. A reluctance, a pulling back that puzzled him.

Suddenly, from the back of the agency came a loud thud. Something had fallen.

Coffee sloshed onto Eric's shirt. He set the cup aside, ignoring the stain, and hurried toward the records room.

"Anne? Is everything all right back here?"

Anne met him in the long picture gallery, face pale. "Gina fainted."

His pulse kick-started. Maybe this was the opportunity he and Sam had been praying for. "Call 9-1-1."

With a prayer on his lips, Eric rushed into the room to find Gina on the floor. Her body jerked in mild convulsions.

"Gina." He patted her sunken cheeks. "Gina."

No response. He pressed two fingers into the gaunt flesh beneath her jaw. A thready pulse fluttered, fast, faint and erratic.

Anne returned, eyes wide and worried. "What do you suppose is wrong? She didn't mention feeling sick."

Grimly, Eric shook his head. "Gina's been sick a long time. And it's finally catching up with her."

Anne knelt at Gina's side and laid a trembling hand on the girl's shoulder. "What is it? What does she have?"

"An eating disorder, I think. But she denies it."

"Oh, my." Anne's fingers touched her surprised mouth. "Yes, I can see that. She never eats a bite when she's here. And you know how we always have food everywhere."

The food—bagels, doughnuts, cookies—were supposedly to make clients feel welcome, but the staff loved to munch, as well. He'd gained a few extra pounds himself.

"Is an ambulance on the way?"

"Yes. Shouldn't we call her parents?"

Eric pushed up from the floor. "I'll call if you'll stay with her."

"Is there anything we can do for her right now?"

Gina had begun to moan and toss her head from side to side.

"Pray." And with that he hurried back to his office for the Sharpes' telephone number, spoke to a stunned Mrs. Sharpe and asked her to meet them at the hospital in Richmond.

By the time Eric returned to the records room, shaken by the fear and distress in the woman's voice, sirens wailed along Main Street. Going to the front door of the agency, he waved the paramedics inside, apprising them of the situation as they worked over the stricken teen.

In a matter of minutes, an IV dripped needed nourishment into Gina's arm. Her eyes fluttered open. When she saw the commotion around her, she tried to sit up. Strong hands pressed her back down.

"Lie still, hon," the EMT said as she pumped the bulb of a blood-pressure cuff, stethoscope already in her ears. "We're taking good care of you."

"I'm okay," she whispered. "Let me go home."

The EMT glanced at Eric and shook her head. "Sorry, sweetie. You need to have a checkup."

"I called your mom, Gina. She'll meet us there."

"Where?" The frightened teen again struggled weakly to rise. "I'm okay. Really."

Her voice was so weak, her breath came in short puffs, but she still wanted to deny the seriousness of her illness. Eric floundered. This kind of thing was way outside his experience.

And then the sweetest perfume wafted in behind him and Sam was at his elbow. With a huge sigh of relief, he stepped back.

"Thank the Lord you're here," he said, not even considering that others might find the statement curious. Sam would know what Gina needed more than anyone.

The tall, stately model took Gina's hand and held on as the paramedics slipped an oxygen mask over her face, then rolled her to the ambulance.

"May I ride with her?" she asked.

The paramedic did a double take. Sweat from the hot day and exertion beaded his upper lip. "Excuse me. Aren't you Samantha Harcourt, that *Style* model?"

Sam gave him a dazzling smile, using her fame to advantage. "Yes. Now may I ride? She needs someone familiar at her side. Someone who understands what she's going through."

The man hitched his chin. "Climb in and buckle up."

Sam turned back to Eric, the artificial smile gone, replaced by the grim reality of Gina's situation. "See you in Richmond?"

"I'm right behind you."

Four hours later, tired and hungry, Sam joined Eric in the hospital cafeteria for a very late lunch. Eric downed a burger and fries with unabashed male enjoyment while she nibbled a veggie wrap. During the last couple of weeks her appetite had returned to the point where she actually enjoyed the taste of food with a minimum of guilt. Only occasionally did the oppressive thoughts come, and even then, she was learning to cast those aside.

Had God done that for her?

"I hate this."

Eric paused between bites, burger at his mouth. Both dark eyebrows went up. "The veggie wrap?"

He always made her laugh no matter how serious the situation. "No, goofy. I hate seeing young girls fall into the same trap I did. I want it stopped. It's madness."

"Can't argue that."

"There's a beautiful, brilliant young girl lying in there fighting for her life. Do you know she plays piano like a pro? And her science-fair project last year won first in the entire state? And she has a four-point grade average?" Sam had made it her business to learn as much about the girl as possible. "We are losing some of our best and brightest to a destructive mindset that shouldn't even exist."

"You should know," Eric said with a gentle tilt to his lips. "You're beautiful, bright, talented. And it got you."

"No more." She slammed her napkin down, surprised at the surge of anger. "No more. Do you hear me, Eric? I want it stopped."

"I'm with you. What do we do?"

"Before I leave here today I'm going to talk to Gina's parents again. To Gina, too, if she's up to it. And this time I won't back down. She's going to get help. I'll see to it." She'd even pay for it, but she would keep that between the Sharpes and herself. "I know the best places in America, in the world, for treatment."

"Will they listen?"

"Let's go find out." With a determination she didn't know she had, Sam pushed back from the round metal table. Eric shoved the last few fries into his mouth and rose with her.

"When you get fired up, you're ready for action."

"Yes, I am."

Sandals clicking on the pristine white tile, she and Eric traversed the long hallway to Gina's room. Food smells gave way to the antiseptic scent of disinfectants and medication. The frigid air-conditioning had her shivering. Or was that nerves for the confrontation to come?

She tapped softly at Gina's door and pushed it open. In tandem, Gina's parents turned, worry hanging over them like a shroud. Gina lay in the bed, awake. IV fluids dripped into both arms while a nasal cannula shot oxygen into her deprived brain. Her sunken eyes were dull and glassy.

"May I speak with you, please?" Sam asked, heart tattooing a rhythm against her rib cage.

"Sure. Come in." Mr. Sharpe rose from an ugly green chair and offered it to Sam.

She shook her head. "I'm fine, thank you. What I have to say is easier said standing anyway."

"We didn't know," Mrs. Sharpe began. "I'm sorry for the way we brushed you off that day after church."

Sam held up a hand. "No need. I understand. That's why I'm here." She moved close to Gina and took the girl's bony hand. "Gina, I know exactly what you're going through."

Gina stared up at her, expression only mildly curious. She said nothing, and Sam recognized the element of denial, even now in the face of overwhelming evidence.

The evil monster of anorexia wouldn't turn Gina loose easily.

Knowing the battle she faced, Sam's stomach jittered, but she pressed on. "I know, Gina. I *know.* We hide it. We lie about it. But we do it."

"You?" Gina whispered.

"Me. But I'm recovering. *Recovered,* by the grace of God." She glanced at the Sharpes, who listened with everything in their being. "Since I was fifteen years old, I starved, purged, dieted, exercised like a fiend, did anything I could to be thinner and thinner. And then one day I ended up like you. In a hospital. Only I was thousands of miles from home and family."

Eric moved to her side and stood, a quiet, solid presence. Sam's chest filled with gratitude. Opening her soul for someone else's viewing was a scary thing. But if one person was helped by it, it would be worth the shame and humiliation.

Eric's strong, supportive hand rested lightly at her back. She drew strength from him and went on, revealing the dark side of anorexia.

When she finished with her own story, Gina murmured, "But being thin made you famous."

"Maybe. But at what cost? My health? My bones being so brittle that I risk osteoporosis? The chance that I may have a heart attack at thirty?"

She kept the worst inside, the despair too terrible to share, lest she break down. Today, Gina needed her help, not her tears. "I'd give up my career in a minute to get my health back. But it's not too late for you."

Gina's eyes filled with tears. Thank the Lord. Sam was finally getting somewhere. She gripped the fragile hand a little tighter.

"I hate talking about anorexia. Hate it. But I'm telling you because I care. There's help available and I want you to get it. I'll help you get it, but ultimately you have to do the work to get well. I won't lie to you. It's the hardest thing you'll ever do. Much harder than fasting or purging. But I can tell from personal experience, if you'll let Him, God will help you every step of the way."

"The doctor suggested a day treatment center here in Richmond," Mrs. Sharpe put in. "I told him we'd do anything, *anything* to get our little girl well. We didn't know. We didn't realize."

Compassion replaced the anger Sam had felt toward the Sharpes. "Anorexics are good at hiding the truth."

"But we should have realized how thin and sick she is."

Mr. Sharpe's square jaw quivered. "Gina's always been our perfect little girl. Our princess. She was all we ever had. We tried to be good parents."

"Don't blame yourselves." As adoptive parents of an only child, the Sharpes no doubt worried they had failed in some way. Which explained their reluctance to accept Gina's condition in the first place.

As Samantha spoke, encouraging, educating and listening to Gina and her parents, something new and wonderful blossomed inside her consciousness. A hope. A purpose.

Her agent had been after her to appear on *Afternoons with Douglas Matthews,* and though the concept made her nervous, she would accept. But she wouldn't talk about modeling or clothes or other celebrities as Douglas suggested. She would do much more.

Even though she'd modeled for royalty and dated movie stars—all great topics to a talk-show host—

none of them knew the ugly secret she would share with Douglas and his viewing audience. And ultimately the entire country.

Now, more than ever, she wanted to fight the madness that had cost her so dearly. And maybe by doing so, she would find purpose and meaning to her own empty life. If she could make a difference in other girls' lives, accepting her own fate would be a lot easier.

She'd heard Eric talk of his work with children as a calling. Maybe, just maybe, here in this Richmond hospital on a hot August day, she had found hers.

Chapter Thirteen

Application denied.

Eric's living room was deathly quiet. Even Barker sensed the mood and lay at Eric's feet, staring up with worried eyes.

The words from the caller hung in the air like a disease, deadly and unavoidable.

For reasons known only to themselves, members of the South African adoption council had made their decision. Amani and Matunde could not leave South Africa. Eric's application to adopt the boys had been denied.

He'd made four more international phone calls hoping for answers, praying the caller had been wrong. The calls only confirmed his worst fears. The local authorities had ruled against foreign adoptions. Though Eric considered himself as much South African as American by virtue of the years spent in the country, apparently South Africa didn't share his sentiment.

His hope for bringing many of the Ithemba children to America was gone, too. While he might work in other African nations, the one that held his heart and sons was closed.

How would he tell his boys that he could not be their father?

He wandered into the bedroom he and Sam had spent hours decorating. She'd gone a little overboard on their shopping trip, but her glow of pleasure had weakened his protests. With her creative eye, they'd made a perfect room for two little boys adjusting to a whole new world—a safari theme. Sam had even painted a savannah scene of green grass and baby animals on one of the golden-tan walls. Until then, Eric had had no idea she could draw and paint.

He rubbed a hand over his face, squeezing his lips together. He'd known rejection was a possibility, but he'd always thought God would make the adoption happen.

Grown men didn't cry, but if they did… He picked up a stuffed monkey and stared down at it. Amani would have loved this. Guess he should put it in the mail.

Expecting to hear from her agent, Sam caught the call on the first ring.

"Hey." Eric's deep baritone tickled her ear. She closed her eyes against the wonderful sensation. She loved hearing his voice. And hated knowing their time together had to end.

"Hi."

"What are you doing?" He sighed and she detected an element of sadness.

"Waiting on a call from my agent. Is everything all right?"

"No."

A little sprout of anxiety shot up. "What's wrong? Is Gina worse?"

Though she'd visited the hospital alone first thing this morning, an anorexic could put her life in jeopardy in a matter of hours.

"It's not Gina. I talked to her folks. She's really down and not talking much, but she isn't worse."

Sam breathed a sigh of relief. Now that she knew her purpose in life, she wasn't willing to lose one girl to the monster.

"Then what's wrong? You sound awful."

"I need to see you. Can I come over? Or would you come here?"

Sam faltered. Last night at the hospital, she'd decided to end things with Eric. But just hearing his voice brought back the indecision.

"I'm really kind of busy."

"Oh. Okay. Well…"

Silence hummed in her ear. She couldn't stand knowing he was hurting. "What's wrong, Eric? Talk to me."

"My petition to adopt Amani and Matunde was denied today."

"Oh, no. Oh, Eric." Her heart sank to her freshly pedicured toenails. "That's horrid."

"Yeah."

Again that hum of silence, the heavy weight of his sorrow stealing the energy from him. She'd never heard him so low.

"Want me to come over?"

"Would you mind?"

This was the man she loved. He needed her. Eric Pellegrino didn't normally need anyone, but he needed her. No matter that they had no future; they had today. And today the man she loved needed her.

"I'm on my way."

When Eric opened the door, Sam walked straight into his arms and held him like a broken child.

"I'm sorry. I know how much you love those boys."

"Yeah," he murmured against her shampoo-scented hair, relieved to share his heartache with someone who knew Amani and Matunde. He had friends, but none of them had met his boys. Sam had. Sam loved them, too.

And if he were truthful, the only person he wanted to be with tonight was Sam. She was the partner he wanted by his side when life hurt.

For a long time, while Sam held him and he soaked in her love, they said nothing at all. No words were needed. She understood. That was enough.

Though he wanted to stay in her arms forever, when several more minutes passed, Eric sucked in a deep, shuddering breath and stepped back. Automatically, his hand found hers and held tight. He needed the connection desperately tonight.

"Let's sit. Want something to drink?"

She shook her head. "No. I want you to be okay."

"And I want my boys."

They went into the living room and sat together on the fat brown couch. Still holding his hand, Sam scooted around to face him, knee to knee.

"What happened? Do you know what went wrong? Did they give you a reason?"

"The local authorities decided to end foreign adoptions. Period. The ball was in their court and they said no. End of story."

"Can anything change their mind?"

"Nothing I or any of the people I work with know about."

"I'm sorry." His dog ambled in and collapsed at their feet with a low moan. "Even Barker seems depressed."

Eric's mouth quirked. "He is. I promised him two kids with enough energy to throw his stick all day long."

"What can I do to cheer the two of you up?" Sam's silvery eyes reflected his own sadness.

"Being here helps. I needed you, Sam. Thanks for coming."

She glanced down at the dog and swallowed. "Maybe I should take you somewhere fun to get your mind off things. Would you like that?"

He shook his head. "Maybe another night. I'm not in the mood to enjoy much of anything. Tomorrow's float trip will be hard enough."

After the Noble Foundation Picnic, they'd promised to chaperone a group of the teens on a canoe trip down the James River as reward for all their hard work. Normally, he loved doing that kind of thing, but tonight the outing sounded more like a burden.

"I'd forgotten about that."

Sam's tone echoed his hesitation. Did she feel the loss of Matunde and Amani as deeply as he did? Or was there something else going on? She hadn't wanted to come over tonight either, but after hearing the reason, she'd agreed.

"We promised the kids. We gotta do it."

"Do they know about Gina yet?"

"I haven't talked to anyone. With this coming down today…" He let the thought trail off.

"Tomorrow will be important then. They'll need our counsel, yours especially. You're the missionary disguised as a social worker."

The joking reference to the day they'd played hide-and-seek with the media brought a smile. He'd kissed her that day and several times since. And with every moment and every kiss, he fell more and more in love with Sam Harcourt.

She'd admitted she cared for him. Was that the same as love?

"You were pretty amazing with Gina and her parents. Degree or not, you knew what to say and do in a very touchy situation."

"Experience is a good teacher. Unfortunately, I've had more experience in that realm than I care to think about."

* * *

They talked on. About Gina. About Sam's decision to use her personal battle in a crusade against eating disorders. About the float trip. And most of all, with bittersweet memories, they talked of Amani and Matunde.

Sam understood the loss much better than Eric imagined. He'd lost his children. So had she. Only he could have more. She couldn't.

The reminder crashed in as it always did, warning her that a Christian did what was best for the other person. And the best thing for Eric was to find a woman to love him and give him the children he wanted. Especially now that he'd lost the boys.

As much as the thought of Eric with someone else pained her, it was the right thing to do.

Tomorrow was absolutely the last time they'd be together as a couple. They'd have a great day, laugh together with the kids, and when it was over, she would cool their relationship. A little at a time, she'd let him go. After tomorrow.

Chapter Fourteen

Eric thought he might actually survive.

In the Saturday-morning sun, he and Sam walked across the concrete parking lot to the Youth Center. He hadn't slept much last night, having spent most of the night praying and trying to understand, but this morning he didn't notice the lack of sleep.

He credited a lot of that to the woman at his side.

Last night she'd been there for him. They'd even prayed together, an act that had thrilled him to his soul. The hurt of losing his sons would take a long time to heal, but with Sam by his side, he would make it. He only hoped his boys would be all right.

Not that he intended to completely give up. He would file an appeal and write letters to the South African government.

He reached for Sam's hand, pulled her against his side. On the way to the youth center, she'd been telling him about her plans to appear on *Afternoons with Douglas Matthews*. He knew how hard the decision had been and he was incredibly proud of her.

"Douglas Matthews has a big following. You can reach a large audience and do a lot of good. You'll be awesome."

"I'm anxious about it," she admitted, raising big gray eyes to his.

"Understandable. But the talks you've had with my Sunday school class were a huge hit."

He gazed down at her, thinking of the way she'd openly discussed her eating disorder with the Sharpes and then come to his rescue last night, putting her own worries aside. Sam Harcourt was a lot more than a pretty face.

Today she reminded him of the first time he'd seen her. Pale hair whipped back into a ponytail and covered with a hot-pink baseball cap. Khaki shorts with a hot-pink T-shirt tucked neatly into the waistband. She wore no jewelry other than a pair of small black-and-silver earrings.

"A television show is a lot different," Sam said, still fretting about the upcoming appearance.

"You're accustomed to the lights and cameras."

"But not to sharing my shortcomings and failures with total strangers."

Their athletic shoes reverberated in the long, empty hallway. From inside the main meeting room, a chorus of voices could be heard. The kids were already here and raring to go.

"You didn't fail, Sam. Don't think that. Failure would be not using your experience to help others."

She squeezed his waist. "Thank you. You're a big reason why I decided to do this."

"Yeah?" He liked the sound of that. He liked everything about Sam Harcourt.

The realization that he was in love with her filled him with happiness. After years of prayer and waiting on the right woman, he'd found her. His instincts in Africa hadn't failed him. The Lord had sent the love of his life all the way across the ocean and then orchestrated their meeting again here in Chestnut Grove. Eric didn't believe either meeting was a coincidence.

Nikki, Tiffany and the other kids stopped talking the moment the adults walked in. To forestall the usual round of moon-eyed glances, Eric dropped Sam's hand.

This morning the kids had more than matchmaking on their minds, however. Two of their own were missing. Jeremy and Gina.

"How's Gina?" they asked all at once.

"We heard she passed out," Tiffany said, a chocolate doughnut in hand. "And you took her to the hospital."

"What's wrong with her?" Nikki demanded. "Is it bad? Is she dying? Her mom wouldn't let any of us talk to her on the phone."

He supposed they should have called the kids yesterday and filled them in, but he'd had a few other things on his mind.

He held up one hand. "Hold on and I'll fill you in."

Even though he wanted to protect Gina's privacy, he knew she would need the help and encouragement of trusted friends. He gave a brief rundown of Gina's eating disorder, encouraging each one to be supportive in the coming days and weeks. The kids listened, their jovial mood replaced with a more somber one.

"Scary," Billy said when Eric finished talking. "Why do girls do that?"

"It happens to boys, too," Nikki said. "I read about it. Not as often, but it happens."

Billy looked as if he didn't believe a word. "Weird."

"I get hungry just talking about it," Dylan said, his joke lightening the mood a little.

"Should we call off the float trip?" Nikki asked.

Eric shook his head. He'd expected that question and had even considered it himself. "No point. Gina's getting great care and she'd feel terrible to think she spoiled your day. The best thing we can do is go on with our plans." He held up a digital camera. "And take lots of photos to share."

By the time the ten teens and two adults arrived at the Float Shop, the mood of adventure had returned. In advance, each pair had packed an ice chest and picnic lunch in preparation for the three-hour canoe trip.

Sam had volunteered to prepare a picnic for herself and Eric. In exchange he had furnished the small ice chest of drinks. Sam had lovingly made Eric's favorite Virginia baked ham and Colby cheddar sandwiches and had even included a pack of his favorite peanut-butter cookies. She might even eat one, too. Today was meant for fun with Eric and the teens, and she planned to enjoy it to the max.

Along with a half-dozen other adventurers, they loaded the shuttle and headed toward the launch site. On the way, a guide gave out instructions for safety and proper handling of the boat.

When they reached the river, the summer sun glistened on the slow-moving water. They'd purposely chosen one of the easy float trips for safety concerns, although most of the kids had paddled canoes before.

Manned with a river map and wearing life jackets, they separated into pairs. An air of suppressed excitement simmered through the teens. Occasionally, one of them cast a funny look at another and they'd both grin. Sam wondered, but decided they were still matchmaking.

Poor kids. They had no clue.

Sam questioned her motives for coming today. She'd promised the kids after the Noble Foundation Picnic that she would accompany them on this float trip. At that time she hadn't known all that would transpire to this point. Now that she was here with Eric, listening to his wonderful laugh, watching him tease the kids and draw out even the most timid, her heart hurt like crazy. Eric was too fine a man, too special, too everything to be stuck with her.

Putting on her model's smile, Sam said, "I think we're ready."

"Everybody have their equipment?" a guide asked, checking and rechecking.

At the chorus of nodding heads, Eric swept a hand toward the rows of waiting boats.

"Choose a canoe, guys, and mount up." He rubbed his hands in anticipation. "Time to get the party started."

En masse, the group headed for the shoreline. "You first, Eric. We'll help you and Sam cast off."

"Can't refuse an offer like that."

Sam reached for the ice chest but Dylan whipped it away. "I got it. You jump in."

"Why, thanks, Dylan. I appreciate that."

The boy responded with a moonstruck grin she recognized too well. Even though these kids had spent lots of spare time with her, they still reacted as if she were special.

As Eric helped Sam into the tottery canoe, the teens gathered around. All wore silly, puzzling grins.

One of the older boys leaned over to brace the boat. "Watch your step."

The boat tipped sharply and Sam gave a nervous laugh. "Am I sure I want to do this?"

"Chicken?" Eric asked, eyes dancing.

She pointed at him. "You're going to eat those words, Pellegrino."

Holding to either side of the aluminum boat, she gingerly positioned her body at one end while Eric took the other, facing her. An oar in each hand, he used them to push against the shore while Billy, Dylan and the other boys sloshed through shallow muddy water, and with one mighty shove, launched the canoe toward deeper water.

Cries of victory went up as Eric and Sam floated away from shore. With strong muscled arms, Eric smoothly guided the boat.

"Come on, guys," he yelled to the kids onshore. "We can't wait all day."

But instead of heading to their own boats, the teens began a celebratory round of high fives, whooping like victors at a hometown football game.

What was going on?

"No need to wait," Nikki called, waving. "We're not coming."

"What?" Eric stopped paddling. "Come on now, quit fooling around."

"No fooling. We're going for burgers. Be back later." One of the older boys jangled the car keys high above his head. "And don't worry. Caleb is meeting us in town."

"Caleb knew about this?" The boat drifted farther from shore while Eric and Sam sat in stunned inactivity.

"Yeah. I think it might have been his idea." Nikki's kohl-rimmed eyes sparkled. "He canceled our reservations. You and Sam have fun."

And before either Sam or Eric could further protest, the teens hopped back on the shuttle. Grinning faces pressed to the windows, they waved as the bus pulled away.

For a minute Eric and Sam sat unmoving in the

small boat. Given her decision, Sam didn't know whether to laugh or cry. But she had to hand it to those kids. When they set their minds to a task, they were amazingly creative.

"I think we've been had," Eric said, still wearing that stunned expression.

"And beautifully done, I might say."

"Did you see this coming?"

"Not at all."

"Me either."

They floated along in silence for a few seconds. The other boaters had pulled away by now and a rumble of distant voices drifted over the softly rippling water.

"Do you want to go back?" Eric asked.

"Do you?"

"There won't be another shuttle down here for at least an hour."

"I guess we're stuck." Although *stuck* was not the way she ever felt with Eric, she wondered about the wisdom of spending an entire afternoon in a romantic canoe with a man she loved but shouldn't encourage.

Eric glowered, but his chocolate eyes twinkled. "Not sure I like the way you said that."

She relented. "You know what? We're here. The weather is beautiful. Might as well enjoy it."

"My sentiments exactly." He dipped a paddle into the water. "So sit back, m'lady, and enjoy the ride."

"I can help paddle. I'm not a total wimp."

As she reached for an aluminum paddle, Eric gave

her a fierce stare. "And ruin my reputation? No way. Wimp or wonder woman, it doesn't matter. I paddle. You provide the inspiration. Just like in the movies."

They grinned at each other across the length of boat. And Sam thought why not. Why not relax and have fun together? Life afforded few enough days as beautiful as this. And Eric desperately needed the distraction that physical exercise and the beautiful setting could provide. She couldn't give him much, but she could give him today.

"I haven't been in a canoe since I was a teenager," she admitted, leaning toward him, hands folded over her knees.

"The last boat I paddled was a leaky old wooden canoe with my oldest brother, Shane. We were bass fishing in a watershed lake."

"Catch anything?"

"Considering that I was ten years old, I can't say I remember. I do remember Shane chucking me overboard once and tossing me a float ring."

"Seriously? Your brother pushed you out of the boat?"

White teeth flashed. "I was a pain. He had a girl-friend. Mom made him take me along as chaperone."

"Wise mother."

"Not so wise if Shane had drowned me."

"Did you tell on him?"

"Are you kidding?" He looked aghast. "Brothers don't squeal. Besides, if I had, he would have drowned me in the kitchen sink."

They both laughed at the silliness.

"How did you survive two brothers?"

"And don't forget the sisters. I'm the baby. They made me play dolls when I was too young to know better. My brothers never let me live that down."

They talked on, sharing childhood stories. Sam seldom talked this candidly with another human being. Never with a man. As the big sister, even with Ashley she was always guarded to a certain degree. In the crowd she frequented there was always the jockeying for position, the posturing, the facade. But with Eric she could be the real Sam Harcourt.

The morning breeze over the river was a whisper. The soft *splish* of paddle against water and the lap of crystal current against the canoe was gentle, restful music. Samantha breathed in the humid, fertile scent of summer from the thick Virginia forests lining the shore.

After a bit, they floated, sometimes paddling, sometimes not, but always talking, talking. Sam leaned back in the slender boat, stretching in the warm sunshine, content to listen to Eric's deep baritone all day.

Eric loved his family. That much was clear. He was a family man all the way to his soul.

Sam trailed her fingers in the cool water, wishing, dreaming, but knowing wishes didn't come true. Was she playing with fire? Too weak willed to make the break when she knew good and well they could have fun, but no future?

The phrasing grabbed her. That was her life. Sam Harcourt, successful cover model. Fun but no future.

Her gaze drifted to Eric. Strong hands gripped the

paddles; broad shoulders flexed as he stirred the water. Beneath a tattered baseball cap, his darkly tanned skin shone with a light sheen of perspiration. All man. That was her Eric.

Her Eric. Dangerous thoughts. Other than a friend, he could not be her anything. Not forever anyway. She wasn't that selfish.

By now they had made a bend in the river and not another boat was in sight, only more trees and thick, tangled underbrush.

Eric brought the paddles inside and let the canoe drift. A dragonfly buzzed low over the boat, hovering as if curious about the people aboard. Gossamer wings glistened in the sunlight.

Eric leaned forward to waggle the toe of her tennis shoe. "Can you imagine what it was like for the first settlers who saw this place?"

She sat upright. They'd come to a narrow slice of river banked with heavy, close-growing timber. The hardwood trees cast a dark shade over the water and blotted out the sun.

"Scary probably. They had no idea what was in those woods."

"Brave souls to venture across an ocean to an unknown world."

"Very scary. No shopping malls."

Her joke brought a quirk to his always eager-to-smile lips. He glanced at his watch. "Nearly noon. Hungry yet?"

"You've done all of the paddling. You must be starved."

"If you don't feed me soon, I won't be able to row you home."

Maybe that wouldn't be such a bad thing. To stay out here on the secluded river alone with Eric and never have to deal with the real world.

"There's a little island up ahead." She pointed at one of the many small islands dotting the vast river. "We could go ashore and have a picnic."

"Sounds good. Two castaways on *Gilligan's Island*. Hope there aren't any bears."

She feigned horror. "Why did you have to say *that?*"

Chuckling, Eric waggled his eyebrows and took up the paddles once more. With biceps flexing beneath the short sleeves of his white T-shirt, he turned the boat in a wide arc. He paddled close to the bank and Sam hopped out, grabbing the tow line. He followed, and within minutes the boat was secured to a willow weeping into the water.

Near the edge where she stood, tiny purple flowers covered a small clearing. Birds chattered in the scraggly pine trees and insects buzzed amid the low-growing tangle of Virginia creeper. The little island was pretty in a wild and rugged way.

"I forgot to bring a tablecloth," she said. "Nowhere to sit."

Eric stripped off his life vest. "We can sit on these."

"Brilliant." She peeled off the uncomfortable vest and tossed it onto the ground.

Eric was already on his haunches, pulling sandwiches out of the insulated picnic bag. He handed her one. In exchange, she handed him a soda from the ice chest and took a bottle of water for herself. They ate in hungry silence for several minutes.

After a while, Eric said, "I didn't think I could possibly enjoy today."

"Are you?"

"Yeah. It's your fault, too." He tossed the last bite of ham-and-cheese into the air and caught it in his mouth.

"Always have to blame somebody, don't you?" she joked.

But despite the teasing words, Eric was serious. He dragged the makeshift chair close to her side. "You're good for me, Sam."

She didn't dare return the compliment. Not here on this isolated and decidedly romantic island.

"I want to ask you something," he said softly, seriously.

Sam's pulse skittered. "If more shopping is on your agenda, I'm your girl."

"Are you?" he asked. "My girl?"

The word *yes* formed in the back of Sam's throat, but she trapped it there.

Taking her water bottle, she leaped up and said, "This place is beautiful. Let's explore."

Eric's look was puzzled, curious, but he pushed up, dusted his hands down the sides of his camouflage shorts and followed.

When he captured her hand, she gave up the fight. She could no more resist Eric today than she could swim the length of this river.

"You want to explore the woods?" he asked, eyeing the dense underbrush ahead.

"Probably not. Bears, you know."

"And chiggers." He scratched at an imaginary bug bite.

They made a turn and sauntered around the edge of the island near the water. Insulted frogs leaped into the shallows at their approach.

Eric pointed at a felled tree. "Beavers have been here."

They stopped to investigate and Sam perched on the downed birch. Dying leaves rustled with the sudden downward movement. She looked up to find Eric standing above her, one hand braced on an adjoining tree trunk.

Her heart fluttered in response to the intense look in his chocolate eyes. If only…

Before she could finish the thought, Eric dipped as if to kiss her. She stopped him with fingers pressed to his lips. If he kissed her today, she might forget her resolve.

"We need to head back."

Again that quizzical expression. "Did I do something?"

"Of course not. Never." That was the last thing she wanted him to think. "It's my fault."

"What's your fault?"

Everything. But she didn't say that. Instead, she leaned forward to push at the tangle of grass and brambles rubbing her skin. "My legs are getting scratched."

"Ah." And then his serious mood passed and he squatted beside the log. "Piggyback ride back to the boat?"

She shook her head. "Silly."

"Come on. Let me play the hero." He backed toward her and patted the tops of his shoulders. "Hands right there and off we go."

He would always be her hero, and she would never forget this lighthearted, lovely day. Refusing to regret one moment of joy with Eric, she climbed onto his back and clung like a monkey.

He took off in a gallop, intentionally bouncing her around. Once he headed straight for an overhanging limb, but at the last minute dodged sideways to miss it. Her laughter blended with his and echoed out across the deserted island.

When they reached the picnic site, he knelt like a camel. As she dismounted, Sam patted the top of his head and said, "Good horsey."

"What? No tip?"

"Sorry, the service wasn't that good."

"The least you could do was feed me another cookie."

"Glutton." Sam poked the peanut-butter cookie between his teeth and began collecting their belongings.

When Eric helped her into the boat, he held on a little longer than necessary, smiling softly into her eyes.

Her rib cage expanded with the interesting mixture of contentment and anxiety. If only today could last forever.

He took up his paddle and this time she joined him, eager to work off lunch. Funny that she'd eaten two cookies and hadn't even counted the calories.

"I wonder where the kids are?" Eric asked.

"Probably back at the center still congratulating themselves."

"I'm glad they pulled it off."

"Me, too." She'd always have the memory of today.

"Even if I do this?" He flipped a few water droplets in her direction.

"Bully." She dipped her fingers into the water and returned fire.

"Wimp." He pulled the paddle into the boat and shook the droplets in her direction. Then, grin mischievous, he scooped a handful of the James, threatening.

Sam backed as far away as possible, which wasn't far in the small canoe. "Don't you dare."

"Dare? Did you say *dare?*" Flinging the water away, he came toward her. The boat rocked from side to side, but Eric was a sure-footed sailor, balancing perfectly. He loomed over her. "My middle name is *dare.*"

Shrunk up into her end of the boat, Samantha laughed and slapped at the water, ineffectively splashing them both.

Eric lunged. At the same time, Sam feinted to the left to escape. Without considering the consequences, she dipped under his arm and sprang up behind him. Eric spun and the narrow canoe rocked wildly. Arms out to each side, Sam flailed in the air looking for a handhold and finding none.

"Oh, no!" she cried.

And just as she thought she would go overboard, two strong arms caught hers. After a precarious moment while the boat teetered and Eric fought to maintain balance for both of them, they tumbled down, sitting hard on the damp floor of the boat.

A wave, caused by the near mishap, washed overboard. Sam yelped at the sudden slosh of cold water against her skin, heated from the warm day.

"You okay?" Eric's face was so close she could count the gold flecks in his eyes. A glint of humor danced in their depths.

"I thought we were going for a swim."

"We still can," he said, teasing.

"You first."

He laughed. His warm breath, smelling sweet from the cookie, brushed over her mouth. She suppressed a shiver, both dismayed and intrigued to discover how quickly her mind went from taking a cold plunge to longing for a warm kiss.

"You have mud right here." He touched a place along her cheekbone, the calloused bed of his fingers a pleasant contrast to her carefully tended skin.

He studied her face thoroughly, as if she were a work of art. The tilt of his mouth intrigued her, playful, tender, quizzical.

In the depths of his amused eyes, she saw something else.

Her blood started to hum, a special melody that

only played when Eric was this close. She should move, should disentangle her arms from his, should scoot back to her end of the boat, but she didn't.

"Eric," she said softly. "Maybe we should—"

But before she could finish the thought, his lips closed over hers. Her heart bumped hard against her ribs. Something exquisite and tender washed through her as Eric's strong arms held her and his fabulous mouth kissed her.

She reveled in the moment, letting her own feelings flow out. She had traveled the world and made a small fortune, but in Eric she found what she needed most. Someone to love.

Now that it was too late.

With great reluctance, she ended the sweet kiss. But Eric didn't let her go. Heart in his eyes, he watched her.

"I love you, Sam. So much. I want—"

Suddenly afraid, realizing her mistake, she placed her hand over his mouth to stop the flow of words that would break both their hearts. He'd been moving toward this moment all day. She should have realized as much. Maybe she had. But she had no better idea of how to handle it now than she had last night.

In usual Eric fashion, he nipped her fingertips, then turned her hand over and kissed her palm. Her heart turned over with it.

"I love you, Sam," he said again, very serious now. "I've loved you since that first day in Africa."

Her brain chanted, *No, no, no.* Not now. Not when she'd already set today as her last special memory of the man she'd fallen in love with. Oh, how she wanted to admit she loved him, too. To forget the reason why she couldn't. But she wouldn't do that to Eric. She loved him too much. She also knew what he would do if she shared her secret now. In his knight-in-shining-armor manner, he would say it didn't matter. Sam knew better. Eric wanted a house full of kids. He deserved to have his dreams come true. Letting him settle for less would be the most selfish act of all.

"No," she murmured and watched his happiness fade. Watched hurt and disappointment take its place. "You can't love me. I can't love you." How did she explain without lying? At a loss, she said, "I'm sorry." He would never know how much. "But it's impossible. We can't. I can't."

Eyes glued to hers, he slowly loosened his hold and leaned away. "Are you saying you don't have any feelings for me? Because I'm going to have a real hard time buying that."

Everything in her wanted to tell the truth, that she was crazy about him. That she wanted to be with him. That she'd give up her career, her money, anything to be the woman he thought she was.

Instead she said, "I care for you, Eric. You know that. We're friends, but love, well, I'm not ready for love."

And she never would be.

"I don't believe you. Come on, Sam. Talk to me. What's going on? Why the sudden change of heart?"

She wasn't ready for that question, either. Insides trembling, she looked away, staring into the glimmering wake of the ancient James. She hated herself. Finally, she grasped the only acceptable excuse. "My work. I need to get back to it."

Which was true in a sense. Her career screamed for attention and without that platform of celebrity, who would listen to her crusade against eating disorders?

"Your work? Modeling?" Bitterness edged his words. She knew without a doubt that her answer verified his original impression—that she was every bit as shallow as he'd thought.

She fought down the fire of sorrow threatening to spill tears enough to capsize the boat. Years of pretending to be fine took control.

"My agency is howling for me to get back to work, and Style Fashions is pressing me to do more appearances. There's no room in my life for a serious relationship. I'm sorry if I gave you the wrong impression about…us."

"Sorry?" He looked at her another long, painful minute while overhead an osprey cried. "Yeah. So am I. Real sorry."

And then face set like stone, he took up the paddle and brought them back to reality.

Chapter Fifteen

Eric felt like an idiot.

The Sunday lunch crowd filled the Starlight Diner with lively chatter while smells of home cooking tantalized the senses. Normally, Eric enjoyed coming here after church. Today, however, he'd come alone instead of with friends. The last thing he wanted to do was socialize and pretend everything was all right.

He'd made a fool of himself. How could he be so stupid as to think someone like Samantha Harcourt would choose him over the lifestyles of the rich and famous? Just because he'd led her to Christ didn't mean she'd fall in love with him.

But he thought she had. He thought she felt the same. She gave every indication that he was someone special.

Her words echoed in his head. Friends. She wanted to be friends.

No thanks. He had plenty of friends. He wanted

a partner, a love, a mother to his children, as well as a best friend.

But hadn't she once claimed to want those things, too? Had he totally misunderstood her?

Sandra Lange sashayed over to refill his tea glass. Eric nodded his thanks.

"Something wrong with the roast beef?" she asked, her kind eyes studying his nearly untouched plate.

"It's great." He tapped his belly. "Not too hungry today."

"Uh-oh. Problems?"

He blinked up, taking in her familiar monogrammed blouse and pink apron. Being a bachelor, he ate here often and considered Sandra a pleasant acquaintance. But she wasn't close enough for Eric to share his heart trouble.

"I'm fine. Thanks for asking. Maybe a carry-out box for later?"

"Sure thing." She winked and zipped away, filling tea glasses as she went.

In the back of the room, directly in Eric's line of vision, Sandra stopped to chat with a table of familiar faces, one of whom was his co-worker and Sandra's biological daughter. Kelly had been stolen from Sandra as a newborn by Barnaby Harcourt and adopted illegally. Ever since it was discovered that Sandra was Kelly's mother and her biological father had been the former mayor, Sandra and Kelly had formed a nice friendship. But Eric sometimes wondered about the ache Sandra must carry in her heart for missing out on raising her only child.

Like the one in his heart for Matunde and Amani.

Kelly was joined by Anne Williams, Meg Talbot Kierney and Leah Cavanaugh. If their laughter was any indication, they were in a much better frame of mind than he was.

He turned his attention to a James Dean poster.

Yesterday at the river, Sam's kiss had said she cared for him. But her words had said she didn't. He'd known all along her career was important, but she'd also claimed to be restless and dissatisfied with the lifestyle. Reevaluating, she'd said.

His mouth twisted in self-derision. Apparently, she'd finished the evaluation and decided to go back to the bright lights and the big city.

"Eric. Hey, buddy, what's going on?"

Ross Van Zandt slid into the booth opposite him.

Ross was a friend, but today Eric wasn't in much of a mood for talk, nor was he good company. He should have gone directly home from church instead of coming here. But he'd hoped the surroundings would cheer him up. They hadn't.

"Nothing much." An understatement. His entire life was on hold right now. Sam and the boys no longer part of the future he'd dreamed of. "How about you?"

"Came to pick up my wife, but as you can see, she's not quite ready to go home and put up her feet. They're planning a baby shower for Rachel."

Kelly was a strong and independent woman. Eric thought it a bit odd that her husband would have to drive her home from a meeting with friends, unless…

"Is something wrong? Something going on at the agency I don't know about?"

Ross frowned and ran a hand over his perpetual five-o'clock shadow. "Nothing definite, but I stopped by earlier to make sure the building was secure."

"And was it?"

Ross nodded. "It was. But I had an eerie feeling, as though someone was watching, waiting."

"Did you see anyone?"

"Only Florence, but that's pretty normal. She prefers to polish floors when the offices are closed."

"Understandable." Although the cleaning woman was not Miss Congeniality, she was efficient and dependable. "Kelly hasn't gotten another threatening letter, has she?"

"No. Thank the good Lord. But this undercurrent of hostility from some unknown force feels like déjà vu all over again."

"No clue yet to who's responsible?"

"None." Ross's jaw tightened. "But they'd better walk softly around Kelly. I won't allow a repeat of last time."

Eric had no doubt the private investigator was not just blowing smoke. He'd do whatever it took to protect his pregnant wife. Whoever the troublemaker was had no idea how formidable an opponent he could face.

Before Eric could comment further, the door to the diner opened and all thought of the agency problems flew out into the afternoon sun. Ross's voice faded into the background noise of the busy diner as Sam, with her sister and nephew, entered the diner.

Drop-dead gorgeous in some kind of gauzy print dress and high heels, Sam didn't see him right away. But he couldn't take his eyes off her. Ashley said something to Sam, who nodded, and the pair of women started toward the empty booths behind him.

Heart in his throat, Eric didn't know where to look. What to do. How to react.

He considered a quick trip to the men's room, but before he could make his excuses to Ross, Sam spotted him. Her perfect smile faded. Something— was it pain or his imagination?—flickered across her face. She faltered, slowing. Then, short of outright rudeness, she had no choice. She stopped at his table.

"Eric," she said softly. "Hi."

"Sam." He swallowed, at a loss. What did you say to a woman who'd broken your heart?

Her eyes searched his. "You okay?"

Pride made him say, "Great. Couldn't be better."

She shifted, as uncomfortable as he was. "Well, nice seeing you."

At his curt nod, she whirled away, disappearing to the farthest corner out of his line of sight. He blew out an audible sigh.

Ross cleared his throat. Eric had all but forgotten the private investigator.

"That was weird. And uncomfortable. I thought you two were a hot item."

"Past tense." Eric's jaw tightened with anger. "Her career got in the way."

"Her career? Wait a minute. She told Kelly she planned to cut back on her schedule and work from here. In fact, I think *settle down* were the words she used."

Interesting.

"I guess she changed her mind. About me anyway."

Ross shook his head. "I don't know. It doesn't add up. She and Kelly were talking about babies, of course." He grinned. "That's all Kelly talks about anymore. And Sam said she longed to have a family of her own but didn't know if it was possible."

Eric narrowed his eyes, puzzled. "What did she mean by that?"

"I figured you'd know better than I would. According to the grapevine—" Ross's grin deepened "—mostly a bunch of teenagers who volunteer at the agency, Sam's crazy about you."

"I thought she was. Or maybe it was only wishful thinking because I was crazy about her. Still am."

"Maybe it's my suspicious detective nature," Ross said, "but the conversation between Sam and Kelly was very recent. Like this week. At the doctor's office. How could she change her mind that fast?"

"Sam didn't say anything about seeing a doctor." Was she sick? He looked toward the back of the room, trying without success to see her. It would be just like Sam to hide a terrible sickness from him, to spare him. Hadn't she hidden the anorexia from everyone she loved?

His mind went crazy with possibilities. She was so thin. What if she had cancer or some other terminal illness? Wouldn't she try to spare him? Wouldn't she bravely go it alone?

"Woman's doctor," Ross said, bringing him back to reality.

"Oh." One of Ross's comments kept fluttering around the edges of his mind like a bird beating against a windowpane. If she wasn't sick, and yet she'd told Kelly a few days ago that she wanted to settle down in Chestnut Grove, what had changed her mind?

The day of Sam's appearance on *Afternoons with Douglas Matthews* dawned rainy and muggy. After fielding a call from her agent, three from Matthews's staff, and still another from the advertising guru of Style Fashions, she'd chosen an outfit she hoped would suit all of them. Style wanted her in their clothes, of course, and expected a healthy dose of free publicity.

The television program was broadcasting live from the Starlight Diner. Douglas Matthews and his staff were smart. They knew very well the down-home, nostalgic appeal of the 1950s-style restaurant. If the show was indeed trying to impress the networks, this program could very well do the trick.

The small diner was always busy, but today it was jammed with people. A section of the diner carried on with business as usual. Waitresses and customers looked on with bug-eyed curiosity at the other side, which had been cordoned off for the live interviews. Outside the large windows, passersby peeked in, waving or offering the peace sign in hopes of being on TV.

From previous experience, Sam knew the general workings of a program like this. The crew had spent all morning in preparation, filming promo pieces and intros. She, fortunately, had missed out on all that. Her part was brief. Show up a little early for the mike check, look nice, plug Style and talk. And with the Lord's help, her talk would be the start of something important.

In a beehive of activity, a production crew set up the sound and video equipment, checking and re-checking with multiple tests. A gaggle of staffers and fans fluttered around the charming talk-show host, who seemed to love the attention.

Sam, who had been on television before, was not overly impressed with all the hubbub. Celebrities like models and movie stars were ordinary people doing a high-profile job. The real heroes of the world were men like Eric who sacrificed fortune and comfort for the sake of others.

Moving deeper into the noisy diner, her gaze drifted to the booth where she'd last seen Eric. When she had glanced up to see him there, looking exactly as she'd felt, she'd nearly crumbled.

She'd wanted so badly to sit down with him and pour her heart out. To explain that she'd broken it off not because she didn't love him, but because she did.

Sam forced a smile, lest some camera catch a candid shot of her melancholy. After noting that all staffers were busy, she headed toward the talk-show host himself.

Douglas Matthews, one hand in his slacks pocket, now stood talking to *Gazette* reporter Jared Kierney. Sam figured Jared was writing a story on the popular talk-show host and the persistent rumor that his program was about to go national. According to her agent, the rumor was true and that was why *Style* wanted her to appear. It was also why Douglas had asked her. The "hometown girl made good" angle meant for strong ratings.

As she approached the men, Jared was saying, "The *Gazette* thought you might be interested in airing a program in conjunction with the series of articles I've been working on."

Matthews tilted his golden head, a perfect component to his artificial tan. She had to hand it to the man. He was nice-looking with a certain charisma about him.

"And what series would that be?"

"The one on Tiny Blessings Adoption Agency," Jared answered. "They've gotten a bad rap because of misdeeds that occurred long ago. Together we could bring the truth out into the open."

Matthews's charming, capped-toothed smile evaporated. "I wouldn't be at all interested, Mr. Kierney."

"Why not? The public is fascinated by the stories. Combining our audiences would be an excellent deal for both of us, as well as for Tiny Blessings."

Douglas's blue eyes went arctic. His hands fisted at his sides. "I said no. And I mean no. Adoption is a private matter. Reporters and private investigators should stop sticking their noses into other people's private lives."

Before Jared could say more, the talk-show host whirled and stalked off. The fawning staff members closed around him immediately, but he barked out, waving them away. Surprised at the uncharacteristic behavior, they shrank back.

"I don't think he appreciated your suggestion," Sam said.

Jared raked a hand through his hair, expression speculative. "No kidding." And then as if he had only just recognized her presence, he added, "Hello Sam. What are you doing here?"

"I'm on the show today."

Jared's eyebrows shot up. "Score one for Matthews."

Sam didn't comment on that. "I wonder why he was so rude. Your idea was a good one."

He shrugged. "Everyone has an opinion about the adoption scandals. Now we know his."

Sam considered that good news. At least Douglas wouldn't question her on screen about the Harcourt family's part in all the trouble.

"I don't think I've met your friend," she said, smiling at the pretty brown-haired woman standing silently next to Jared.

"My apologies, ladies. Sam Harcourt, meet Lori Sumner. Lori is a colleague of mine at the *Gazette*, a crack reporter. If I don't watch out she'll have my job." He smiled to let them know he teased.

The women exchanged pleasantries and then

Sam asked, "Are you going to be working here in Chestnut Grove?"

"Some," Lori said. "When Jared is on other assignments. I'm really interested in the adoption issue, which is why I came along today. I'm in the process of adopting a little girl myself. We were hoping to convince Matthews to let me work with his staff on a mutually beneficial program. Maybe several if the public responded well."

"I don't think that's going to happen."

They all looked toward the talk-show host, who had regained his composure and was chatting amiably with a man wearing headphones around his neck.

"Miss Harcourt." A bespectacled woman carrying a clipboard approached her. "I'm Phyllis, Mr. Matthews's assistant. He's asked me to make sure you have everything you need. It will be a while until you're on. Would you like to wait in Mr. Matthews's dressing trailer? It's very comfortable, air-conditioned with all amenities. We could have lunch brought out to you."

Matthews had a dressing trailer? Unusual for a local program.

Besides, the red-carpet treatment in front of friends made Sam uncomfortable. "No need. I'm with friends."

"As you wish." The woman flashed a smile. "But let me know if you need anything. Please have lunch, drinks, whatever you want. The show will pick up your tab. And that of your friends, of course."

Sam returned the smile. "Thank you, Phyllis."

As the young assistant walked away, Sam said to her companions, "Do the two of you have time to keep me company or are you off to another story?"

"Actually," Jared said, face alight with mischief, "since Matthews is paying, let's grab a booth. I'm thinking filet mignon."

The two women laughed.

"We'll teach him to be rude to nosy reporters."

A quick look around revealed no empty booths or tables, and as they were about to give up, Jared nodded toward the back. "Pilar's brother is sitting down at the end. He won't mind sharing his booth with two beautiful women and one hungry dude. Come on."

Although Sam hadn't met Pilar's brother, she was friendly with Pilar and her police-officer husband, Zach. Pilar was a stunning Latina beauty, and her brother Ramon bore the same dark good looks.

At their approach, snapping black eyes looked up from a plate of pasta. Immaculately groomed in a tailored suit, the handsome Ramon Estes no doubt turned many heads. From Lori Sumner's expression, hers might be one of them.

"Jared. Ladies." Ramon's gaze settled briefly on Lori before returning to Jared, eyebrows raised, waiting for an introduction.

"Ramon, do you know Samantha Harcourt?"

Even though the space was limited, Ramon politely rose and, one hand holding his jacket closed, almost bowed. Yes, indeed. His Old World manners served him well.

"Only her pretty face." Ramon's smile flashed white against his dark skin. "A pleasure, Miss Harcourt."

"Sam, please."

"Sam it is." His attention drifted back to Lori and rested there. Interested, Sam thought. "And this is—?"

"My colleague, Lori Sumner. She's—"

Before Jared could complete the introduction, Ramon's interested expression dissipated. His lips flattened to a straight line.

"Lori Sumner?"

The room temperature dropped ten degrees.

"Have we met before?" Lori asked a bit uncertainly.

Eyes as hard as onyx, Ramon bit out, "I'm representing Yesenia Diaz."

When Lori only stared at him, befuddled, his nostrils flared. "Yesenia Diaz, the biological mother of Lucia Diaz. I'm her attorney."

Lori went deathly pale. She grabbed the table's edge. "What are you talking about? What do you know about my daughter?"

"*Yesenia's* daughter, Miss Sumner. She intends to reclaim her child. And I'm representing her in that action." He whipped a card from inside his tailored jacket. "Perhaps you should give me a call." He edged out of the booth. "If you'll excuse me. I have to get back to the office. Nice meeting you, Sam."

And then he was gone.

So much for Old World manners.

Lori, shaking like a palm in an earthquake, slithered onto the vinyl seat. Sam quickly summed up the situation and slid in next to her. Jared took the other side.

"My baby. He wants to take my baby away," Lori said in a broken whisper.

"Can he do that?"

"I don't know. I didn't even know the mother wanted Lucia back. No one at the agency mentioned anything like this."

Sam wanted so badly to call Eric. He would know. She patted Lori's arm, then rested her hand over the reporter's shaking fingers. They were as cold as Ramon Estes's eyes. "Do you have an attorney?"

"I didn't know I needed one. The agency was taking care of the adoption details, and last I heard the mother wasn't even in the picture. I don't know what I'll do if they take Lucia away. She's my whole life."

"How long have you had her?"

"Three months." A tremulous smile. "She's so precious."

Sam's heart ached for the woman. Memories of Ashley's battle to regain custody of Gabriel flickered through her head, a story Lori most likely did not need to hear right now.

"Do you have a photo?"

Lori nodded and took a handful of adorable baby pictures from her purse.

The child was clearly Hispanic, and Lori was not. Surely, in today's world the difference had nothing to do with the legal action.

"She's beautiful." Sam searched for other comforting words, glancing to Jared for help. He leaned forward to speak but as he did, someone called Sam's name.

·"Miss Harcourt, we're ready for you."

In her concern for Lori, Sam had forgotten to be anxious about the upcoming interview. Now her butterflies returned in hordes.

In the next few minutes, the whole world would learn her ugliest secrets.

Chapter Sixteen

Remote in hand, Eric flopped down in a fat brown chair and channel surfed. Barker flopped down on the floor next to him, baleful eyes staring at the food-laden coffee table. Next to an open bag of Cheetos was a half-empty bag of Eric's favorite peanut-butter cookies and a six-pack of soda. Comfort food, his mother called it. Eating junk to elevate his mood. He was having a pity party.

A missionary and a social worker should know better.

He crammed a whole cookie into his mouth and crunched.

Sam and Gina had starved themselves, and here he was overindulging.

Not a pretty picture.

Images flickered across the plasma TV. The DVD was primed to record. Might as well admit it. He'd taken off this afternoon to watch Sam's interview. As much as he prayed for all to go well, he still felt lower than a snake's belly.

"Glutton for punishment," he muttered. He popped the top of a soda and took a long, fizzing drink that burned the back of his throat.

Sam was nervous about sharing her story with the world and he wanted to pray her through it. A man didn't stop wanting good things for a woman just because she didn't love him in return.

But she did. She *did* love him. He knew it as well as he knew his own name. And yet, she'd broken things off. And her reasons didn't add up. He'd phoned her after the talk with Ross, left a message on her cell, but she'd never responded.

"It's over, Pellegrino. Adjust."

Her reasons didn't add up because he didn't want them to. End of story.

Barker raised a bored eyebrow. When Eric said no more, the dog sighed and closed his eyes.

The theme music of *Afternoons with Douglas Matthews* filtered from the surround sound. Eric's gut tightened. Sam would be on there in a few minutes.

Expectantly, he listened to the opening teaser that promised an exclusive interview with Style fashion model, Sam Harcourt, followed by the inevitable commercial.

He crunched another cookie.

The doorbell rang. Barker shot up from the floor like a Roman candle and charged the door, yapping like mad.

"Quiet, boy," Eric said as he shoved off the chair to answer the bell, cookie crumbs flying.

FedEx delivery stood on his tiny porch. Eric took the large brown envelope, thanked the man and returned to his chair, turning the packet over to read the label.

"Africa," he said to Barker, who was now cleaning up the spray of cookie crumbs.

With the new adoption program finally under way in several African countries, he had so many documents coming and going from the continent he assumed this was more of the same. Here was the only bright spot in losing the boys. At least his work would take him to South Africa several times a year to see them and to make certain they had everything they needed. It still hurt knowing they would never be his official sons. But they would always be the sons of his heart. And he would father them from a distance.

He still didn't understand the Lord's direction in this thing. He'd been certain he was supposed to adopt them. But then, he'd also thought God had sent Sam into his life.

Maybe someday he'd go back to Africa and live with the boys again. If the Lord willed.

He ripped the seal and withdrew several official-looking documents. Eager to get back to the TV program, he quickly scanned the letter.

And then he read it again slowly.

After the second read-through, he barely breathed. Did this say what he thought it said?

He tried again, and the third time was the charm.

He let out a whoop loud enough to send Barker into another fit of barking.

"Look at this." He waved the paper in front of the dog's startled face. "We did it. We got it. They changed their minds." He held the document toward heaven. "Thank you, Lord."

Indeed, the letter was an official invitation for Eric Pellegrino, former missionary and trusted friend of the children of Africa, to return for the adoption of Matunde and Amani Mbuli.

Official. Not a phone call. A signed, sealed, delivered letter of approval. The real deal.

He rifled through the rest of the packet, determining the travel date and other details. It was going to happen this time. It was really going to happen.

After the show, he'd call the boys. They'd be as ecstatic as he was.

After the show.

His attention drifted back to the television screen. Doug Matthews's toothy mouth smiled at him. Any minute Sam would appear.

Sorrow momentarily overrode his excitement. Sam would be happy. She would want to know. Maybe he should call her.

Maybe not.

At that moment, the camera focused on Sam. Eric could practically hear the ratings clickers going crazy. Dressed in trendy Style fashions, bangles on her arms and ears, blond hair flowing around her sculpted face, she added a layer of sophistication the local show had never achieved. She reminded Eric of the stars he'd seen on the late-night talk shows. Knowing Sam the way he did now, she didn't even realize her power.

During the first part of the interview, Sam shared her thrill at being named the Style girl and answered Douglas's questions about the places she'd been and the famous people she'd met. Though he knew she was nervous, Eric didn't think anyone else would notice. Her class and gentle humor served her well.

But then Matthews gave her the opening she must have been waiting for. "I understand you've taken on a platform, Sam, a sort of crusade. Will you tell us about that?"

Sam grew serious. She swallowed, and Eric suffered an attack of jitters on her behalf. He sat forward, pinched his upper lip in concentration.

"Help her, Jesus."

Then in a soft voice filled with passion, she began to speak. "There's a terrible myth being perpetrated upon young women in our society. The myth of thinner, prettier, richer. I'm here today to combat that myth. To stop the madness. I'm talking about eating disorders, anorexia and bulimia."

"I imagine you see a lot of eating disorders in your profession."

"I do," she said. "But the problem isn't confined to certain professions or locations or even to one type of personality."

"Are you saying anyone can fall victim?"

"Anyone, Douglas." She leaned forward, silver earrings catching the light. "Most of us had core issues, problems that we didn't know how to handle, but the main issue with an eating disorder is control. Girls who feel out of control, for whatever reason, tend to control the one thing they can. Their weight."

"You keep saying 'we,' Sam. Are you trying to tell us something?"

The camera zoomed in for a close-up. Sam blinked several times and took a deep breath. "A month ago I would never have admitted the truth. Not to my friends. Not to my family. And certainly not to a television audience."

"You're anorexic?"

"I doubt it's much of a surprise, though we like to think we're hiding the disorder from everyone. But, yes. My problem started when I was fifteen and got worse over the years. I knew there was something wrong with me, but I couldn't stop. And I was ashamed to tell anyone. That's what I want to say today." She looked directly into the camera. "If anyone watching needs help, ask for it. Please. People will understand. I brought an 800-number hotline to call. Stop denying you have a problem. Get help before it's too late. The long-term effects of anorexia, even if it doesn't kill you, are terrible."

The camera cut back to Douglas, who spoke to his audience with compassion and concern. "The number is on the bottom of the screen. Call if you need help." Then he turned his attention back to his guest. "Tell us more, Sam. Talk about the problems anorexia can cause."

Even from the confines of his living room, Eric

could feel the hush that had descended on the diner and the show's live audience. The beautiful, successful, totally together model had everyone's attention.

"I'm not a medical expert. I can only speak from personal experience and from watching what has happened to some of my friends. Anorexia and bulimia are cruel taskmasters. They control your life, your every waking moment, and in the process they eat away at your insides. Once the disorder takes control, the chemical changes in the body affect the brain and distort thinking, making it impossible to make rational decisions about food. Mood and personality changes occur. Friends and family are shunned because we're so afraid they'll find out and stop us. And the weird thing is this, Douglas. We think we're right. We really, truly think we're too fat."

The camera moved to wide angle showing Sam's tall, slender form.

"But you're very thin."

Sam's smile was sad. "Not as thin as I have been but I'm one of the lucky ones. I got help." She shook her head. "No, wait. I'm not lucky. I'm blessed. For years I fought the disorder through treatment and counseling. Don't get me wrong. They help and anyone with anorexia should seek professional help. But the battle of distorted thinking still raged in my mind all the time. The negative thoughts."

"What happened? Why are you willing to talk about this now when you hid it before?"

"God," she said simply, and Eric felt a burst of

pride. It took a lot of strength to do what Sam was doing. No wonder he loved her so much. "I found a relationship with the Lord Jesus Christ. I wouldn't be here today if that hadn't happened.

"I also stood at the bedside of a teenage girl who could have been me ten years ago. I felt God prompting me to do something. He's blessed me with a job in the spotlight. It's only right that I use my public voice to make a difference.

"For a long time I thought God was angry with me, but a very special friend helped me understand the truth. God loves me no matter what, but He wants what's best for me, too. And that's for me to be healthy, to take care of the body He blessed me with."

"Which gets us back to the question. What exactly can occur if a woman continues the path of bulimia and anorexia?"

Sam paused, and Eric saw a tiny muscle twitch beneath her eye.

"Go on, Sam. You're doing great."

When this was over, he'd send her some roses with a card, whether she wanted to hear from him or not. His heart nearly burst with pride. She was some kind of woman.

"There are several long-term effects," she said. "None of them nice. Brittle bones and osteoporosis. Damaged internal organs." Her voice dropped to a thoughtful murmur. The cameraman reacted with a close-up. "The most awful, to me, is infertility."

A beat of silence invaded the set. Douglas Matthews knew how to milk the timing.

"You're saying anorexia can prevent a woman from having children?"

Sam swallowed again. Moisture gathered in the famous gray eyes. "An anorexic can do so much damage she either can't get pregnant or her body can't sustain a pregnancy if she does conceive. Either way, she's lost her chance to ever have a baby with the man she loves."

The last words were spoken in a stark whisper. Though she'd spoken in couched terms, the devastation on Sam's face said it all.

Eric sat up straight, heart pounding so hard, he was sure Barker could hear it. A dozen recent memories flashed through his head.

The doctor's visit Sam hadn't mentioned.

Him, yammering on and on about his desire for a big, noisy family.

Her reaction at the baby dedication with all the pregnant women and babies and kids. Since that day he'd felt her pulling away.

Blood roared in Eric's ears as the truth slammed down like a heavy cellar door.

Sam couldn't have a baby.

It wasn't that she didn't love him. It wasn't that at all.

His beautiful, tragic Sam knew his desire for a family and rather than ask him to give up his dream, had chosen to break off their relationship.

Could that be it? Or was this only wishful thinking on his part? Either way, his Sam was hurting.

"Oh, Sam." He squeezed his eyes shut and began

to pray for guidance. What should he do? How did a man handle a situation like this one? She didn't want him to know.

He pushed off the easy chair and walked around the living room, still praying.

Finally, he stopped stock-still and stared at the envelope on his coffee table. His boys' future was at stake here, too. They deserved every good thing he could give them. And the best thing of all would be a mother and father to love them forever.

If Sam loved him, and he believed she did, she was trying to protect him.

There was only one way to find out.

He grabbed his keys from the end table and took off in a dead run.

Chapter Seventeen

Sam stepped off the makeshift dais to murmurs of both concern and congratulations. Her knees quivered from exhaustion, her body weak with fettered emotion. She felt totally drained, but she had done it. She only prayed the Lord would use her words to touch lives, to save lives.

"Great show, Sam," Douglas said. "The networks will love this one."

His comment bothered her. "I hope more than the networks are affected. I didn't come here to boost your ratings."

For a second, he looked taken aback but just as quickly, the host gathered his wits and said smoothly, "Of course. That goes without saying. I'm all about making a difference."

Somehow the words rang hollow, but frankly, she didn't care. His show was the vehicle she'd needed to get the message out. The first of many. Now that she'd begun, she wouldn't stop until the madness was conquered.

The tiny bell over the diner door jangled and Eric burst into the room. With a fierce look of determination, his gaze locked on hers and he strode toward her.

Sam's heart jumped. As emotionally rent as she was, seeing Eric was a soothing balm. She wanted to run to him and let him hold her. Just hold her and let her rest her head against his strong shoulder.

The people standing around looked on in curiosity. But the clatter of plates mixed with the activity from the TV set had started up again. Voices rose and fell, but Sam neither saw nor heard anything but Eric.

His dark, slashing eyebrows plunged together as he zeroed in on her. She stood, waiting, yearning, blood pounding in her ears.

Something in the way he moved, the way he stared, sent a warning to her exhausted mind. Had he watched the show? Had he somehow read between the lines and learned her cruelest secret?

Please Lord. Please don't let him know.

Eyes never leaving her face, Eric stopped in front of her, posture tense. Sam swallowed hard, her mouth going as dry as cotton.

After a few anxious beats, he took her arm. "I need to talk to you. Please."

He gave the few onlookers a hard stare meant to warn them off. It did. "Excuse us."

"Eric, what's going on?"

He didn't answer. Just stepped so close no one could possibly overhear. "You can't have a baby, can you?"

Pain seared through her like a hot knife. She jerked back. "I can't believe you asked me that."

"Tell me." Jaw like granite, he insisted, "Tell me the truth."

"It doesn't matter. It doesn't change anything."

"It does matter. It matters more than anything in the world." He stabbed a finger at his chest. "You're killing me, Sam. I have to know the truth."

At the harshly whispered words, Sam squeezed her eyes closed. "I never meant to. I wanted to protect you. I didn't want to give you false hope."

His sorrowful brown eyes pierced her very soul. "If you can say you don't love me, I'll walk away and never bother you again. I won't like it, and I'll die a little, but I'll walk." He took her chin in his hand and forced her to look at him. "Tell the truth, Sam. Do you love me?"

The exquisite contrast of tenderness and calloused fingers melted her. This strong, masculine man was laying his heart on the line. He was taking a chance on her. Couldn't she take a chance on him, too?

"You know I do."

Hope flared. "Say it again."

"Don't be cruel, Eric. You know love isn't enough."

"You're wrong. The Bible says love is everything. If you love me the way I love you, it's all that matters."

"But it isn't. You want a family. It's your greatest dream." She fought the tears and lost. They spilled over.

Eric's thumbs caught them. "Don't cry, sweetheart. Please don't cry. We can have a family."

She shook her head, pulling away from his seductive touch. When he was this close and so incredibly sweet, her resistance disappeared like smoke on wind.

"Yes, we can. We already do." He pushed an envelope at her. "Amani and Matunde are coming home. By Christmas."

She glanced down at the envelope and then back up at him, incredulous. "Seriously?"

Eric allowed a smile. "Yes. I don't know how or why, except God, but the South African government has granted me special status to adopt them."

"Oh, Eric, that's wonderful news!" She threw her arms around his neck in a celebratory hug. And then she caught herself and stepped away again. "But that doesn't change things for us. I'm glad about the boys. You'll never know how glad, but you want more, Eric, and I won't stand in your way."

"I want a houseful of kids, Sam. I don't care whether they're adopted or biological. If God gives them to us, they will be ours. A child born in the heart is no different than a child born of the womb. God calls it the spirit of adoption. Don't you see, sweetheart? The world is full of children who need an incredible mother like you. God adopted us to be his children because he loved us. We can do the same."

Myriad emotions shifted through Sam. Confusion, sorrow, fear and finally a small flickering flame of hope. "You don't care? Are you sure you wouldn't hate me in a few years because I can't give you a baby?"

"I've always dreamed of a big family. But for the last year my dreams have been about you. You, as the mother to Matunde and Amani, and to all our other children, regardless of where they come from. You, Sam. By my side as my partner and love. No one else will ever do. I love you, Sam Harcourt. Only you."

Sam's resistance crumbled. She took one step toward him, reaching out. With a tender smile, Eric took her hand in his and fell to one knee.

"Maybe I need to do this right," he said, and his beloved eyes begged her to agree. "Marry me, Sam."

"Oh, Eric," she whispered. "I love you so much."

"Is that a yes?"

She nodded, afraid to trust her voice any longer. Tears ran down her cheeks, though now they were tears of relief and joy.

Eric slowly rose to his feet, holding tightly to her hand. Sam's heart beat a happy response. When he pulled her into his arms and kissed her, the sweet seal of promise was like coming home.

Sam forgot where she was, forgot everything but the pure delight in knowing Eric loved her enough. For the first time in her life, she was enough.

So when a disembodied voice yelled, "Cut," followed by applause, she felt disoriented.

Eric lifted his head, keeping her snugged close to him, as they looked around. He wore the same dazed look she was certain reflected on her face.

"I think we've drawn a crowd," Eric said.

Sure enough, the entire diner looked on, smiles wide. A cameraman stood by, camera pointed in their direction.

"Did you get all that on tape?" Sam asked, fearful of what they'd heard.

"Only the proposal. The TV audience will love it."

"What if we don't want to share?"

"Too late. We were live."

"Live?"

The cameraman nodded. "Beautiful stuff. I'll make you a copy."

Eric and Sam stared at him and then at each other. After a stunned moment, they both laughed and went right back to kissing.

* * * * *

Be sure to pick up
A MOMMY IN MIND by Arlene James,
the third book in the
A TINY BLESSINGS TALE *continuity.*
Available September 2007
from Love Inspired.

Dear Reader,

I am delighted to be part of the TINY BLESSINGS TALE series from Love Inspired. Thank you for joining the adventure! Writing the story of beautiful, broken model Samantha Harcourt was right up my alley. I love the reminder that God is no respecter of persons, that He is far more interested in who we are on the inside than in who we appear to be to the world.

To everyone who has written or e-mailed about my Love Inspired books, I want to say a special thank-you. You'll never know how important it is in this solitary business to get feedback from readers. I love hearing from you either through my Web site at www.lindagoodnight.com or c/o Steeple Hill, 233 Broadway, Suite 1001, New York, NY 10279.

Have a wonderful summer—and stay tuned for the next installment of A TINY BLESSINGS TALE.

Your sister in Christ,

Linda Goodnight

DISCUSSION QUESTIONS

1. What was the primary theme of *Missionary Daddy?* Can you find parts of the story to substantiate your answer?

2. How does Eric's childhood relate to his initial misjudgment of Sam?

3. What happens in the story to change Eric's view of Sam?

4. Sam struggles with an eating disorder. What is your view on eating disorders? Are they a cry for attention, a distorted body image, a spiritual problem or something else? Explain.

5. How does Sam change and evolve in the story? What events trigger the changes? Can you pinpoint specific examples?

6. What is your view of international adoption? What about interracial adoption? Is there scriptural basis for your answers?

7. Do any of the characters remind you of someone you know? Who and why?

8. What are some of the things Sam kept hidden inside? Do you think women should keep some things inside, or let them out? What does Scripture say about this?

9. Who do you think is causing the problems at Tiny Blessings Agency?

10. Do you think adoption records should be opened or closed? Does a mother who gives her child up for adoption have a right to keep that secret from the world? What about the child's right to know his birth parents? Which is more important?

REQUEST YOUR FREE BOOKS!

2 FREE INSPIRATIONAL NOVELS
PLUS 2
FREE
MYSTERY GIFTS

Love Inspired®

YES! Please send me 2 FREE Love Inspired® novels and my 2 FREE mystery gifts. After receiving them, if I don't wish to receive any more books, I can return the shipping statement marked "cancel." If I don't cancel, I will receive 4 brand-new novels every month and be billed just $3.99 per book in the U.S., or $4.74 per book in Canada, plus 25¢ shipping and handling per book and applicable taxes, if any*. That's a savings of 20% off the cover price! I understand that accepting the 2 free books and gifts places me under no obligation to buy anything. I can always return a shipment and cancel at any time. Even if I never buy another book from Steeple Hill, the two free books and gifts are mine to keep forever.

113 IDN EF26   313 IDN EF27

Name	(PLEASE PRINT)

Address	Apt. #

City	State/Prov.	Zip/Postal Code

Signature (if under 18, a parent or guardian must sign)

Order online at www.LoveInspiredBooks.com

Or mail to Steeple Hill Reader Service™:

IN U.S.A.: P.O. Box 1867, Buffalo, NY 14240-1867
IN CANADA: P.O. Box 609, Fort Erie, Ontario L2A 5X3

Not valid to current Love Inspired subscribers.

Want to try two free books from another series?
Call 1-800-873-8635 or visit www.morefreebooks.com

* Terms and prices subject to change without notice. NY residents add applicable sales tax. Canadian residents will be charged applicable provincial taxes and GST. This offer is limited to one order per household. All orders subject to approval. Credit or debit balances in a customer's account(s) may be offset by any other outstanding balance owed by or to the customer. Please allow 4 to 6 weeks for delivery.

Your Privacy: Steeple Hill is committed to protecting your privacy. Our Privacy Policy is available online at www.eHarlequin.com or upon request from the Reader Service. From time to time we make our lists of customers available to reputable firms who may have a product or service of interest to you. If you would prefer we not share your name and address, please check here. ☐

LIREG07

Love Inspired®

TITLES AVAILABLE NEXT MONTH

Don't miss these four stories in September

SOMEBODY'S BABY by Annie Jones
Josie Redmond had raised her twin sister's baby as her own, and now the child's father was in town seeking his son. But when Adam Burdett saw Josie with little Nathan, he discovered it wasn't just his child he was interested in.

A MOMMY IN MIND by Arlene James
A Tiny Blessings Tale
A tiny baby stole Lori Summer's heart and made her petition to adopt. Before the papers were signed, though, the teenage mother changed her mind. The teen's lawyer Ramon Estes believed in his case, but longed to get to know his opposition in a more personal way.

A TREASURE OF THE HEART by Valerie Hansen
She needed stability, so Lillie Delaney headed to her tiny hometown to find it. But everything there had changed. She turned to Pastor James Warner for guidance, only to find a handsome motorcycle riding rebel who showed her that the Lord does indeed work in very mysterious ways....

LOVE'S HEALING TOUCH by Jane Myers Perrine
In the busy hospital emergency room, Dr. Ana Ramirez admired orderly Mike Fuller's quick skills and impressive bedside manner. So she proposed a simple cup of coffee to talk about his future, never expecting to find herself wishing she were a part of it.